Yesterday

Also by Siân James:

ONE AFTERNOON

Yesterday

SIÂN JAMES

COLLINS
St James's Place, London
1978

William Collins Sons & Co Ltd
London · Glasgow · Sydney · Auckland
Toronto · Johannesburg

First published 1978
© Siân James 1977, 1978

ISBN 0 00 221959 X

Set in Baskerville
Made and printed in Great Britain by
William Collins Sons & Co Ltd, Glasgow

I Mam

Chapter 1

I sprinkled sugar on the remains of Toby's poached egg so that he was willing to finish it. I felt better as I took away his empty plate; he'd had his tea, so he couldn't be ill, so I could go out.

'Pretty Toby,' I said, wiping his mouth with a hot, moist cloth so that I couldn't feel his hot, moist face.

'Daddy's going to have trouble tonight if you ask me,' Dora said.

I wasn't asking her. 'Nonsense.'

I put Toby on the floor with his hammer-pegs. I'd heard John at the gate; he hadn't missed the fast train.

As he came in, Dora kissed him with a great show of affection. Still holding her, he knelt down to Toby.

'He's ready for bed. You know where to find his clean nappy if you need to change him. Dora's going to help you get your supper.'

'Off you go, then,' John said, and I ran upstairs to get changed.

It was Friday night, my night out. I ran a bath. Everything was ready, my dress hanging behind the bathroom door; buttons and bows. I'd be out of the house in five minutes unless Dora got weepy at the last minute or Toby had been sick on John. I dried myself and dressed. My face was so brown that I didn't bother with make-up, only some stuff on my eyelashes which are rather fair and sparse; they never see the light of day, poor things, and some grey eye-shadow.

Dora clung to me when I went back to the sitting-room, but didn't cry. 'I don't want you to go,' she said, 'but have a nice time.'

'See you later, then,' John said. Toby looked at me as though trying to remember who I was. As I bent to kiss him, though, recognition seemed to dawn and he handed me a small piece of well-chewed toast.

7

'Thank you, Toby.'

The car wouldn't start and I had to will myself to count a hundred slowly before trying again, and then it did. I'd be on time.

I was meeting him at the station car park. As usual I locked my car and got into his.

'We'll eat first,' he said, without as much as a kiss or a fondle. 'Put the safety strap on.'

It was the first time we'd had a meal together, the first time our weekly meeting hadn't been entirely given over to sex. This is the beginning of the end, I thought; tonight he's going to call it off, his wife has found out, he's got another woman, I don't excite him any more.

'Have you been to Ambleside Mill? No? Good, you'll like it.'

He drove fast down the motorway and off the motorway to one of those unspoiled Kentish villages full of Jaguars and Aston Martins, and insanely fast to the car park behind the large neon-lit restaurant. He took my arm and marched me to the front door.

'Haven't eaten all day.' He looked down at me and smiled for the first time.

The inside of the restaurant was much better than I'd expected, all antique oak; dressers and court cupboards and chests and refectory tables with white table-linen and heavy brass candlesticks. At least he was going to spend some money in disposing of me. He did everything in style.

I tried to feel calm: please let me take it well, I always knew it couldn't last long, not for ever, I've had seven weeks, my whole life is changed. I'll never lose what he's given me, only what good will it do me without him? Please, I mustn't make a scene.

He was still smiling at me but I felt no better for it. I knew he'd be kind.

The waiter brought us a very long menu each, gothic lettering on mock vellum, and I tried to concentrate. When I felt his hand on my knee, I was so surprised that I bumped the table, shaking the cutlery and glasses.

'Sorry,' he said, but without taking it away. Could it be all right?

'Grapefruit juice,' I said. I hadn't been able to concentrate.

'The steak's good here.'

'I'm a vegetarian.'

I breathed deeply. I classify people according to their response to that. 1, Good for You. 2, And what do you do about Shoes? 3, But haven't you heard that Lettuces Scream?

He said nothing at all. Until the waiter came. Then he said, 'Ask the chef, please, what he can do for a vegetarian.' The waiter murmured something about *omelette champignon* being on the menu. 'No, not omelette anything. See what he can manage, please. Fillet steak for me, rare, sauté potatoes, French beans and the wine list.'

'How nice it is to have a meal with you,' he said, leaning over the table and kissing me on the cheek. 'Even more brown, even more freckles. How are your strap marks?' He pulled me towards him and peered down my dress. 'Lovely.'

'Why haven't you eaten today?' I asked.

'Too much work. If I'd stopped for a meal I'd have been late meeting you. I was afraid you wouldn't wait. How long would you have waited?'

He was holding my hand now. 'How long would you have waited?' he asked again. 'Sooner or later one of us is going to be held up, we should discuss where we'd go to wait, we couldn't hang on in the car park indefinitely. Today I was in a panic about it. I wondered if you'd go home, and if so whether I'd dare ring you.'

'You were in a panic?'

'Yes, in a panic. Don't you believe me?' He crushed my fingers in his large hand. 'Don't you believe me?'

'I'd wait half an hour in the car park,' I said. 'After that I'd go to the Chequers in Linfield Road and stay there till closing time.'

'Not the Chequers. It's full of art students. You'd get picked up. The Falcon on the other side of the road is much quieter, much safer for big girls.'

9

'All right, the Falcon. I'll go to the lounge. Only I'll drink an awful lot because of being nervous, so please don't be very late or I'll be sozzled. Will you go to the Falcon if I'm late?'

'Yes. But don't be late.'

'I was almost late tonight. The baby was ill. I've never left him with a temperature before. Perhaps I'll ring up and see how he is.'

'All right. Don't be long.'

So I went to the foyer and rang home.

John picked up the phone at the first ring. Whom was he expecting? I wondered.

'Is Toby all right? Is he asleep?'

'Yes, he's fine.'

'And Dora?'

'She's fine.'

'I just thought I'd make sure. Toby was a bit flushed earlier on.'

'They're both fine. Don't worry about them, for God's sake. They're fine.'

'Are you all right?'

'Of course I am. I'm fine.'

'Good night then, love. See you later.'

As I walked back I was conscious of how intently he was watching me. He wasn't giving me the brush-off after all. Far from it, he seemed to be tightening his hold.

So I enjoyed the meal. I changed my place, came to sit next to him instead of opposite, and kept my leg tightly against his.

He'd ignored my request for grapefruit juice and had ordered asparagus for both of us, and the next course when it came was delicious, a wonderful mixture of tastes and textures, with cream and mornay sauce and tiny mushrooms, and I prolonged it, ate everything including all the vegetables he was leaving, and drank a lot of wine. I was very happy.

When the waiter brought the menu again I looked for the raspberry and meringue gateau the woman on the next table had.

'Raspberry vacherin,' I told him.

'Coffee and the bill, please,' he told the waiter.

He turned to me. 'You've taken too long already.'

I tried to pout but my lips couldn't manage it.

'What now, then?' I said.

He took the bill and wrote out a cheque. We left the coffee.

As we drove back to Hursel Common he wanted to know when I could spend the night with him, which upset me because I knew I'd never be able to arrange it. 'What's so marvellous about a bed?' I asked. 'For God's sake don't keep wanting more all the time.'

'I wouldn't be human if I didn't want more all the time.'

'You know, I thought you were all set to finish with me, tonight.'

He turned to look at me and decided that I was serious. 'I'm glad you suffer a bit.' He smiled as he said it, but for the first time I felt a shiver of apprehension about our relationship, not fear of its ending as I'd felt earlier, but fear of its overflowing on to the rest of my life, capsizing it.

'Let's not get too intense,' I said as he stopped the car in the usual place. Neither of us spoke as we climbed over the fence and walked through the brushwood.

He laid out the rug on the damp grass; it had been raining that day; but he seemed withdrawn as though his heart wasn't in it. He sat waiting for me to join him; usually he spread me out like the rug; so I went to him, knelt by him and opened his shirt and kissed his chest. 'I couldn't do without you,' I said, 'that's all I meant.' I was on the point of tears, it was lovely there, my face on his chest, such a warm secret smell like the roots of flowers.

He turned to me then and we lay down together. He kissed me and I kissed him for hours it seemed, till my body was melting and I didn't know which was my body and which his. We were one again, what he wanted was what I wanted, we had one will, one spit, one juice.

'I panicked because I thought you wouldn't wait for me,' he said.

'I would, I would. I'd go to the Falcon.'

'That's right. Not the Chequers. Oh, what a good girl you are.'

'I'm getting used to you,' I said later.

'Is that good?'

'Oh yes, lovely. I don't mind, now, when you lie away from me and smoke.'

'Where exactly am I away from you?' He pulled me nearer, so that we weren't only touching, but overlapping.

'I don't mind that you're thinking about your work.'

'I'm not.'

'What are you thinking about?'

'The baths I used to go to when I was a boy.'

'Nice?'

'The soap they gave you was so hard it didn't lather a bit, it just scraped you clean like emery paper. You've got such soft skin.'

'Are you thinking about me now?'

'No, just trying to keep you happy. Oh, you've got very soft skin and very silky fur, you really have.'

'If God didn't want people to make love on the Common, why did he invent bracken?'

'And the dark.'

'Do owls mate in the night or the day?'

'When you hear "tu-whit, tu-whoo", it's two owls, did you know that?'

'They're not going "tu-whit, tu-whoo", just "whooo-whooo".'

'Umm. Carole says you're very intellectual, Tessa.'

'Walt says you're a rising young executive. And he's right, my God.'

'Oh, what a good girl you are.'

Yesterday. All my troubles seemed so far away.

Chapter 2

My husband worked for BBC radio. He was an assistant
producer in the Education Department. The job, though,
hadn't turned out to be as interesting as he'd hoped and he'd
gradually become rather bored and embittered. He's very
clever. We were at University together; he was expected to get
a First and did, whereas I was expected to get a Third and
did. He was happier then, he likes being top. Later, he was
always fearful that I was overtaking him. If ever I'd managed
to read something which he'd missed, he'd say I was trying to
steal a march on him.

He liked mixing with the actors and playwrights and direc-
tors he met at the BBC and didn't care much for the residents
of Chestnut Close, Bromley, where we lived. He used to
complain that all the men he travelled to and fro to work with
were in advertising, though they weren't.

We moved out to Bromley when Dora was six months old.
My sister and I had been left five hundred pounds each at the
death of a great-aunt, and my father, who seems to believe
that a good mortgage supplies the necessary ballast for a
marriage, was very keen that I used mine for a deposit on a
house.

John wanted to buy a flat in Holland Park, near the one
we rented, but I didn't think it was suitable for bringing up
a family, and until Toby was born, I wanted a large family.
I saw the development at Chestnut Close advertised in one of
the Sundays, with an architect's impression of a few of the
houses; and architects, with a few strokes of their 2B pencils,
can make anything look like a Swedish hill-top village; and
the price quoted was exactly the one we'd worked out as our
ceiling.

John used to say, later, that he'd disliked the house from the
beginning, but the truth was that he had at least a temporary
enthusiasm for it.

The Show House was closed when we drove out, we saw an unfurnished one which the builders had forgotten to lock, the walls were white and pale grey with all the paintwork white, and the evening sun was pouring in through the ceiling-height windows of the living-room. It looked so large and cool, even the dining-alcove ('the black grilles, a sophisticated feature affording not only an impression of height, but also identification of area') looked attractive without the table and chairs and sideboard which were afterwards to make it look like a very small furnished cage. 'We could have bookshelves all along that wall,' John said, 'I could have my desk here.' It sounded like enthusiasm.

I walked up the staircase and decided which one of the bedrooms would be ours and which one Dora's. 'Every bedroom has a fitted wardrobe,' I told him when he came up a little later, 'think how much money that will save us. Your mother will be able to have the spare bedroom when she comes. The lavatory and the bathroom have got cork tiles.'

Although one of the wardrobe doors fell out as I opened it, I liked everything about the house. The bath and wash-basin were sage green. There was even a downstairs cloakroom.

The kitchen in the flat we rented in Holland Park had peeling brown paint and cockroaches; this kitchen was immaculate, with an impressive array of cupboards and a fitted fridge and cooker included in the price. (There wasn't room for a washing-machine, but I didn't think of that at the time. Eventually we had to get a carpenter to take out one of the cupboards, cutting through the room-length Melamine work-top – a special feature – to do it. Everyone else did the same.)

The only adverse comment John made on that first day was that there was no room for the pram.

'But I can leave it in the garage.'

'At the bottom of the hill! Didn't you notice the row of garages like toy-town as we turned in from the road?'

'I can always leave it in the porch.' (I didn't really intend to.)

'I suppose so.'

(Later, I got used to a porch filled with pushchair, pedal-car, cart, jeep and doll's pram, but at the time I imagined it burgeoning with silvery trailing plants in pretty stone containers.)

We were one of the first families to move in to the second terrace. Carole and Walt had the corner house in the first and had been living there for a couple of months. They invited us to lunch on the first Sunday, which was marvellous because I'd been so busy buying bins and brushes and saucepan-scrapers that I hadn't thought much about food.

Carole is petite and lively with black curly hair. We became friends at once, though John was always bemused at what I found in her.

She did a lot for me.

She came over one evening after work; she was secretary to a firm of interior decorators in the West End; asking whether she could borrow a bain-marie, and when I told her I hadn't got one, and furthermore didn't know what on earth it was, appeared very surprised. 'You look such a wonderful housewife,' she said.

'What do you mean?'

'I mean you look very, very competent, and, you know, very placid.'

'Placid?'

'And you dress so sensibly.'

Dora was eight months old, I was weaning her and was already in an emotional and depressed state, so that at this point I burst into tears, at which she patted my shoulder, poured me a drink and had one herself and waited for me to stop, which I did fairly soon.

I expected her to leave, then, apologizing all the way to the door, but as soon as I'd stopped drying my eyes and sniffing, she resumed the attack.

'Change your style,' she said.

'I haven't got a style.'

'Yes you have. Miss Pinafore Dress – 1962.'

'I'm a size 14.'

'Really. The way you dress I'd have thought 16.'

15

'I can't wear little frilly things like you. I hate buying clothes.'

'I'll go with you. I know a place where they do matronly styles for the fuller figure.'

'I haven't got a fuller figure.'

'Then we'll go to Carnaby Street.'

So the following Saturday I left Dora with John and went up to town with her, but she didn't take me to Carnaby Street but to a certain Hair Salon which I thought was exclusively for film-stars. I didn't want my hair cut or styled or anything, it was shoulder-length and I liked it like that, and I'd never been to any West End Hairdresser let alone that one, but she said she'd made the appointment and that I needn't have it cut unless I chose to, I was the boss wasn't I? But I knew and she knew I wasn't, and if I hadn't been so cross I'd have started to whimper with fright.

And I came out a couple of hours later with no money for clothes but looking and feeling so different that I didn't care. (Even Dora noticed the new me. When I got home she stretched out her hands to feel my short, bright hair and pulled it with all her might and laughed.)

That did it, really, that and being told I dressed sensibly. Afterwards I made an effort and soon didn't even need Carole to tell me which boutiques to go to. Almost overnight I became dishy instead of pretty. It was much more rewarding, and I owed it all to Carole. Carole and I remained friends, though John found her and Walt very boring. In no time at all, he was finding everyone on the estate boring.

When I gave a dinner party for neighbours, he'd never put any effort into it, but would just smile in a superior way and let everyone else do the talking.

When we cleared up afterwards we used to fight.

'Can you think of one interesting remark made this evening?' he'd ask. 'Can you think of one isolated statement during the whole evening which was anything but utterly banal?'

'I don't ask for intelligent conversation all the time. I also like gossip and chat.'

16

'You mean, you actually like hearing about the new rules about rose-hip syrup at the clinic and whether they have enough free expression at Greenways Primary and which swimming pool has the best tea and whether or not Veronica Bailey is going to leave her husband?'

'Veronica Bailey. I didn't hear that. Who said that?'

'She's going to leave dear Roy and move in with Brian Fuller, and if she can tell the difference between them it's more than I can. And Liz Fuller is having Roy. She doesn't mind as long as she can keep the Deep Freeze.'

'Oh, you're making it up!'

'Even wife-swapping would be boring in a place like this. My God, what a choice! Which shall I have? Fascinating Frances, Microbiotic Cookery and Avoid Nappy Rash, or simple Sarah who Makes Her Own, or tiny Trisha with the tiny, tiny mind.'

I finished the washing-up and wiped the draining-board and the work-tops and the table with furious energy. 'You're getting so pompous,' I said.

'Hey, did you hear that the Arkwrights are getting a *bidet*?' He was trying to humour me as he put away the glasses, but I wouldn't have it.

'I wonder if you'd say no to that thin girl with bare feet we met at Oliver Hunt's party. Not that she's likely to be anybody's wife.'

'What exactly do you mean by that?'

'Nothing. She just looks too exotic to be a wife, that's all.'

'You see, you've sunk to the level where you think wives have to be dull and fat.'

'Meaning that I'm dull and fat?'

'I didn't say that, did I?'

That was the sort of exchange we indulged in more and more often. Our marriage was in a precarious state and I worried about it.

In bed that night I thought again about the very thin, bare-footed girl.

A couple of weeks before, we'd been to a party. John had told me, or warned me, that it was likely to be a quite extra-ordinary affair and I'd gone to great lengths to look right for it. The dolly-look never really suited me, I was too tall, my eyes were not round enough, my nose too long. Still, I had silver eyelashes, my hair was cut like a helmet, my new dress, a little crêpe number, purple, was eight inches short of the knee, so I hoped I'd look fairly unobtrusive.

The party wasn't too extraordinary. Maybe some of the people were high, but they just seemed old-fashioned drunk to me and there was so much incense and musk-oil about that it was difficult to tell; everyone seemed, like the lighting, rather subdued.

Then, still quite early in the evening, the very thin girl I've already mentioned suddenly announced that she was going to dance and started swaying about in the middle of the room, moving her arms and her hips and moaning a little from time to time. Several people were watching her with interest if not pleasure, and I was one of them, though in fact I was hardly conscious of her. I was thinking about marriage, and mine and John's in particular. Having a certain amount to drink had given me the courage to examine it in depth, and during the process a small release of breath, a half-sob, escaped me. The very thin girl stopped dancing and with horror I realized that the sob had sounded very like a laugh; a snigger. One or two people smiled quite kindly at me but John's eyes were blazing, so that quite soon I left and went home alone. I had done so before from other parties of his, but never before had he stayed out all night instead of following on a couple of hours later. The next day was a Sunday, he was in the kitchen when I got down for breakfast and neither of us referred to the incident.

However, on the night of our dinner party, after I'd re-introduced the subject, John said, 'What we both need is some time to ourselves.' I was settling down to sleep so I didn't reply, but the next morning asked what he proposed.

He didn't need to give his answer any consideration. 'I'd like to go out on my own one night in the week,' he said, 'and if I go, it's only fair that you should.'

'Fine,' I said, not liking to admit that I couldn't think of anywhere to go or anyone to go with and for good measure absolutely hated the idea. 'Which night would you like?'

We were in the middle of breakfast and that particular day Toby's egg was far too soft. He was playing with it, mixing it up thoroughly in an absorbed and fascinated way, and it was causing me anxiety.

'You can choose,' John said.

The runny egg was suddenly one thing too much. I snatched it away from Toby and put it on the sideboard, whereupon he roared with rage and threw his milk on the floor.

'If Mummy goes out, who'll put me to bed?' Dora asked, bursting into tears. I rushed to comfort her, knelt down to cuddle her, horrified that she should be listening in to the break-up of her parents' marriage, and while I was accessible Toby forgave me and buried his face, and his hands and his egg-spoon, in my hair.

'You can choose,' John said again.

'Shut up! Shut up!'

Then John finished his toast, put *The Times* in his brief-case and kissed us in turn.

'I'm upset as well,' he told me as he went out, and I realized that he was, and at that instant knew that we were in real trouble.

Chapter 3

John and I got married while we were still at University, both
of us fairly, no very, inexperienced.

We were good pals. We laughed at couples who indulged
in jealousies and drama; we were proud that our love was
low-keyed and comforting.

We worked well together. During our Honours year, when
we were married, we hardly went out, we read and studied
and were perfectly satisfied with one another's company.

We had a bed-sitting room that year, a pretty attic room,
but very cold except in the little semi-circle in front of the
one-bar electric fire, and as the year wore on we confined
most of our activities to that area. That's where we studied,
our piles of books a shelter against the draughts from the
doors, that's where we ate our nourishing meals, nuts and
raisins, bread and cheese, Mars and Guinness. Quite often
that's where we slept too, in our separate sleeping-bags, I with
a sweater over my pyjamas and a pair of John's socks, because
the double bed was in the frozen wastes at the other end of
the room. It was in that room that Dora was conceived, in
the summer, though, some time during our exam. month.
I wonder that we had the time.

John got his First and the job with the BBC, and we moved
to London. We had Dora, and after another two years, Toby.
Our sex-life could best be described as comforting, I realize
it now; it was a pleasant thing to do occasionally before we
went to sleep. We had many interests in common.

John, having the better mind, was the first to realize what
a mess we were in.

He had fallen in love with the very thin girl or someone
like her, and had discovered that love wasn't low-keyed and
comforting, but something else. What it was, he didn't confide
to me, but in fairness wanted me to make some discoveries on
my own account.

From the time we made our pact, we were kinder to one another.

I didn't know what to do with myself on the first Friday night so I went to the cinema on my own. The film I saw had had rave notices, but I went to sleep before the end. Toby had been giving me some rotten nights with his back molars, also I was unhappy, which always makes me sleepy.

The following week I asked Carole whether she'd come out with me, but she was immersed in preparations for a dinner party she was giving for Walt's boss and his wife, so I offered to help her with it. I'd done so before, though not for such illustrious guests.

Carole is a very nice girl and bright about lots of things, but she's a nervous cook. She was always saying she could prepare a wonderful meal if only she didn't have to sit down and eat it as well and talk to the guests, when all she could think of was the vegetables drying up and the sauces separating. Walt had suggested that they should take the boss and his wife to a new Italian restaurant in Catford that everyone was talking about, which had hurt her a great deal.

'OK, I'll be your au pair again,' I said, 'I'll dish up and keep everything hot and stir things.'

There wasn't a bit of need for the Yugoslavian accent, I could as easily have been an English mother's help, but the accent turned it into a game. (We had a very talkative Yugoslavian nurse at the clinic, that's why I considered myself an expert at it.) 'Oh, Tessa, have you remembered to heat the plates?' 'Of course I 'eat the plates. Why you think I don't 'eat the plates? In my country we never eat the dinner except we 'eat the plates.' She was too nervous to appreciate my flow of witticisms but they kept me happy.

This time I'd found a perfect dress for the part, a very tight, very brief cotton dress of blotting-paper pink which I'd got for a shilling at the second-hand stall at the market, but Walt still wouldn't let me answer the door. Carole, though, said I could hover in the background to lend tone. At least I saw Walt's boss, fairly impressive, and his wife, fairly dull.

Carole had chosen a menu of formidable complexity; everything had to be tossed, blanched, re-heated, sautéed or stirred. I really worked very hard, but every time Carole came out to fetch something she looked so grateful and doting that it all seemed worthwhile. At least it was better than sleeping in the pictures.

When I was just about finished and trying to make the washing-up last another ten minutes so that I could reasonably go home, even washing the cat's bowl and the electric blender and the salad-holder from the fridge, Walt's boss brought out the tray of coffee cups.

I smiled at him deferentially and he smiled back not deferentially and stayed with his back to the door watching me until I became quite nervous. I went out through the back door to peg a couple of teacloths on the line, but when I got back he was still standing there. If I hadn't known he was Walt's boss and above such things, I would have thought he was trying to chat me up, but then again he didn't say anything.

I kept on wiping the draining-board, at least three or four times, while he still stood by the door watching me. I was finally very embarrassed. When Dora was a baby I could never stop her crying by singing to her, which says something for her musical appreciation, but I could by doing my squint. It's a ferocious squint, and since its success with Dora I do it quite often. I did it then.

But he only went on smiling and showed no sign of leaving the kitchen. 'We will have it over here, please,' I said. He was still holding the tray.

'Are you Italian?'

I decided not to understand the question.

'Italiano?'

'No,' I said at last. 'Yugoslav.'

'Ah yes, of course.' He was still staring at me.

'Well, you're a lovely-looking bird,' he said. 'I hope you've got enough English to understand that.'

'Oh yes,' I said, 'I understand that good enough. Good

night. Goodbye.' I tried to wrest the tray from his hands.

'When can you come out with me?' he asked, without releasing it.

I felt let down by this man. Old Walt admired him so much, revered him almost, and here he was trying to make it with the au pair. I squinted again.

'You're lovely,' he said.

He was mad.

'When?' he asked. 'Please tell me when you'll come. I have to go. When do you have a night off?'

'Friday night only. No more.'

'What time?'

'No more nights off. No more.'

'*Next* Friday then, *next* Friday. What time are you free?'

'Seven o'clock.'

'Good, good. I'll meet you at seven o'clock. The car park near the station. Do you know it? Behind the station. The car park.'

He was talking as people do to the deaf and senile. 'Seven o'clock.' He got hold of my wrist and pointed to the seven on my watch.

I simply wanted him to go. 'Seven o'clock!' I repeated, snatching my hand away.

'Goodbye,' he said. 'Don't be late. Please don't be late.' He was breathing heavily. God, he was mad.

I washed the coffee cups in a fury and it was only after I'd got home that I calmed down. It was me he'd fancied after all, me. Not even dressed in my best, all made up and eyelashed, but just fat old me in a pink cotton dress and sandals, with my hair limp from the steam and the heat.

For the rest of that night I fluctuated between feeling flattered and feeling insulted. Had he offended against class or race? Was he picking me up because he thought I was a cheap, working-class foreigner? Or, on the other hand, because he thought I was plump, pink and nubile?

Perhaps he had loved his nanny when he was a boy. Perhaps

23

he could only relate to the lower classes like the fellow in *She Stoops to Conquer*. On the other hand, perhaps it was just me.

Anyway, it was 1966, the year of the mini-skirt and the Pill and LSD and After Eights, so what was wrong with picking up somebody's au pair in their kitchen.

Of course, I didn't intend to go.

As the next week progressed, I thought perhaps I would go to meet him, just for once. Naturally, I'd tell him about his mistake and perhaps that would turn him right off me, perhaps not. What harm would it do, in any case. The thought of going out with Walt's boss certainly excited me, he was, according to Walt, brilliant; dynamic and ruthless. How I wished I'd listened occasionally when Walt went on and on about him. What exactly was he dynamic and ruthless about? Perhaps I could get something out of Carole. Wasn't his firm something to do with business methods (American?), time and motion studies, computers? Something high-powered, anyway; that was another of Walt's favourite expressions. And he had married, if I remembered rightly, Somebody's daughter, which was another sharp move, Walt said, because the old chap was rolling in it.

By Thursday I knew that I was going to be at the station car park the following night and my only indecision concerned what to wear. Would I have to stick to the tight pink, or could I wear my new brown and cream floral with the cream lace collar and cuffs? Of course I could dress up; he'd expect it.

I knew what else he'd expect, too, but there was no reason at all why he should get it. I had, theoretically, nothing much against the idea. It seemed to me that I was the only person in swinging London, and that included John, who wasn't having a swinging time; but, on the other hand, I wasn't at all sure I wanted it. It was too soon. I wasn't going to be pushed into a sexual relationship with anyone, however exciting, simply because I hadn't got anything much to do with myself on a Friday night.

'Hallo,' he said. 'You came.' He sounded as though he hadn't

24

expected me. He put his arm tightly around me, which was just as well because I felt suddenly faint, my legs heavy as though they were paralysed.

'Here's my car.' He opened the door for me and I got in. As he got in beside me, he gave me one quick look which I couldn't interpret : amusement, triumph, anticipation; before driving off, very fast. I loved his haste.

He was dynamic, all right, no indecision about this one. 'No, you decide', 'I'd like to do whatever you'd like to do', was a thing of the past. I wasn't going to be consulted about anything and my God it was lovely, that's what I felt as I leaned back in my seat and looked at his profile. I'd gone to meet him because I was excitedly curious and because I was lonely, but I felt something else as I sat in the car with him, a strange, singing sensation.

He drove to the Common which he either knew very well or had specially studied for the occasion, to a completely isolated stop only a few hundred yards from the main road.

We didn't speak a word to each other as we climbed the fence and walked through the fringe of prickly trees. He spread out a tartan rug on the grass. We sat down together.

I was surprised at his lack of haste then. He sat looking at me for a long time without touching me, almost as though he wanted me to have a chance to change my mind, to object to being brought out to that lonely place, to protest that I was a nice girl; and by that time all I wanted him to do was to lie on me, blotting out everything except the violent trembling in my blood.

He took my hands and looked at them, turning them over, rather sadly. 'Shall we?' he asked my hands. He spread them out and laid his face in them. He kissed the tips of my fingers.

He sat up and scrutinized me. He stroked my face with great tenderness. He stroked my face and my neck for a long time, very softly and gently, but apart from that he didn't touch me. It wasn't what I expected after the drive out when he'd seemed so sure of himself.

I tried to tell myself that it was just his formula, a tried and tested technique, but it seemed like tenderness, even a sort of homage, the way his hand stroked my face, his eyes never leaving mine. It was strangely healing. It made me realize how much I'd been hurt by John, by what amounted to his rejection of me. It seemed as though he knew it all, though of course he couldn't, and was seeking to reassure me.

So I sat, absorbed in the rhythm of his stroking hands. The sky was pink and full of clouds. Thrushes sang from the wall of trees between us and the path where the car was. Even the clouds seemed tender as petals, but suddenly the thrushes had a note of urgency in their song. I opened the top buttons of my dress and drew his hand downward. It seemed the answer he'd been waiting for to a question I hadn't even considered. Very gently he pushed me back on to the rug.

But no haste, still no haste, but a beautiful slow thoroughness. Kissing became a swooning pleasure, sucking out the honey indeed, a revelation to me of how many different sensations, all gorgeous, one could get from lips and tongues and teeth, biting and sucking, and the long investigation of armpits, navel and breasts.

Oh, it was new to me, and new to me the noise I was making, until it didn't seem a physical thing any more, but the moon on the water, the moon sleeps with Endymion and would not be awaked.

It didn't seem a part of the me I thought I knew, to be making love, out of doors, with a man who was almost a stranger, and pulling him towards me again with desperate little grunts of pleasure, but that was what I was undeniably doing. After some time I felt I had some explaining to do, if only to myself, but I sank back unable to find the right words, or indeed any. His hands seemed intent on confusing me.

'I'm not Yugoslavian,' I said, after several more bright and beautiful minutes, and that wasn't at all what I'd intended to say.

'No, no, you're Tessa,' he said, brushing the hair from my eyes and kissing my mouth before lowering all his weight on to me again.

It seems Carole had been fairly drunk when he'd asked her

26

about the au pair and had confessed that it was her friend Tessa Jilks from No. 14, the best mate anyone ever had, the salt of the earth, and if he wanted to be rude about her best friend's physical attributes then she thought the less of him. It seems he'd had to spend quite a lot of time telling her what beautiful eyes I had and agreeing with her about how extraordinarily kind I was, and what a rare and precious thing friendship was.

The sky had darkened and the thrushes were silent and we lay quietly side by side.

'Do you really think I've got beautiful eyes?' I asked him.

'Oh, yes. And beautiful attributes too.'

Chapter 4

Normal life went on. I was the same wife and mother. (Except that it was like being in the middle of a wonderfully absorbing book which one may be too busy to read except for a little in the evening, but whose characters and events, as well as the fact of its being there waiting to be picked up again, cast a glow on one's whole day.)

So that I took the children to Nursery School and clinic and park and paddling pool and cosy corner in the library, separated them when they fought, when they fell over, comforted them with Elastoplast and fruit-gums, and at bedtime bathed them, read to them, sang to them, kissed them. I also picked up toys from the floor ('now that I am become a man I put away childish things'), shopped, cleaned, washed, ironed, mowed the lawn, weeded the border, picked up toys from the floor, sewed on buttons, watched television, did some reading, listened to music, picked up toys from the floor, cooked many, many meals and waited for Fridays.

'It's Midsummer Eve,' he said as I met him one Friday, our fourth. 'Ring up and say you're going to be late.' I hadn't been out after eleven-thirty before that. 'It's a special night.'

So I phoned John. 'It's Midsummer. I'll be late, probably two or three, do you mind?'

He sounded surprised but said, 'No, I don't mind.'

I felt guilty and miserable in the kiosk, but carefree again as soon as I saw him waiting for me, looking anxious. We drove to the coast.

I'd never cared for cars before, but I really liked the car he had that summer, though I can't remember much about it except the colour, grey and black, and its elegance; it was so unlike our family estate with plastic animals everywhere and pieces of jig-saw and chewed rag-books.

Almost everything is lovely when it's a preliminary to love-making; eating, drinking, dancing, even card games can take on an exciting rhythm, but driving with someone is the best because of the speed and the closeness. I used to watch his face. I got to know all his looks; concentration, impatience, anger, frustration, and the corresponding words; several of his expressions surprised me; before the end of the summer they were springing to my lips though I was careful not to let them pass. All the same I treasured them. (He wouldn't let me kiss or fondle him when he was driving but I loved best of all the look of not-quite-successfully-concealed pleasure when I tried.)

It was nine when we arrived at the sea. He parked the car and we walked and walked and walked along the cliffs to find an isolated spot, but wherever we went there were people with dogs or people with children or people with dogs or old men with pipes or lovers with other lovers.

I tried to tell myself how pretty it all was, the sky; and there was so much of it from up there; full of billowing clouds, Constable would have loved it, and the sea below us, there it was, churning away gently like an oversized Bendix.

It's remarkable how many poems about the sea, most of them with very jaunty rhythms, I know by heart, and I had time to moan through most of them on that walk. 'To sea, to sea, the calm is o'er. The wanton water leaps in sport.' 'A wet sheet and a flowing sea, a wind that follows free.' 'Aye, bury me where it surges, a thousand miles from shore.' 'Now the wild, white horses play. Champ and chafe and toss in spray.' 'The lusty ship of Bristol sailed forth adventurously.' 'Nobly, nobly, Cape St Vincent to the North-West died away.' 'Quinquireme of Niniveh from distant Ophir.' 'I must forth again tomorrow. With the sunset I must be.'

'Let's go back to Chislehurst, for God's sake,' I said at last. 'I can't walk another step.'

But he said, 'Let's go down to the sea to paddle.'

For a second I hoped it was sub-standard Masefield, but he wasn't quoting, he was serious. And that's what we did. We walked and ran and slid down an almost sheer goat- or lemming-track to the sea.

We were far from the town, but the sea was out and there

29

were several people walking on the beach, though we were the only ones to paddle. It was a bright evening, but not warm.

The sea was very cold. He had rolled up his trousers and his legs were white and thin, and at every step I pointed out how brown and shiny mine were and how I was afraid I couldn't fancy him any more, those bony legs sticking out from his rolled-up trousers, he looked like a heron or a comic postcard, and we had our arms tightly round each other, and it was suddenly marvellous, with the setting sun in our eyes.

'We'll come to the sea again.' 'Do you promise?' 'We'll swim together and spend the night together afterwards.' 'How can we?' 'We'll manage it, don't you want to?' 'Of course I want to.' 'Then we will.' 'Do you promise?' 'I promise faithfully.' 'I've got a very sexy bikini.' 'What colour?' 'Apricot.' 'You're all apricot.' 'That's the idea.' 'Why not white?' 'Too obvious.' 'I like the obvious.' 'I bet you've got maroon boxershorts with a diver on them.' 'How did you know?' 'You bought them six or seven years ago when you were slimmer and now you have a ridge of fat resting on the waistband.' 'I haven't got an ounce of fat.' 'What's this? What's this?' 'And I suppose you've noticed that my hair is thinning?' 'Yes, I noticed that the first night I saw you at Carole and Walt's.' 'Are you sure you want to continue our association?' 'I think so; you look fairly distinguished till you roll up your trousers.'

That's about how it went, and that's roughly the point he picked me up and sat me in the sea. I splashed as much as I could but he managed to get right away from me and stood at the water's edge, waiting for me to join him, which of course I had to do.

I started to shiver quite dramatically. I was uncomfortable and annoyed but awfully interested to know what would happen.

'What shall we do now?' I asked him, interested and surprised at the way my voice shook.

I did hope he wouldn't laugh and he didn't but seemed most concerned and subdued. 'I'll get the car and wrap you up in the rug,' he said. That sounded nice.

'But it's awfully far. We walked miles.'

'It's not far, honestly, not from here. I'll hurry. Put my jacket on. Sit here on the wall till I come back.'

He wiped my feet with his handkerchief and made me put on his socks under my sandals. I was still shivering and he was quite ten minutes before coming back with the car. It was beginning to get dark.

He'd got a bottle of brandy and we drank some each, then he drove back to the cliffs, now isolated, and in the dark I took off my wet clothes and he wrapped the rug round me and kissed me and I drank some more brandy and at last stopped shivering.

At about midnight he lit a fire. He really and truly managed to light a fire with only a cigarette-lighter and two double-spreads of *The Times* and some dry leaves and sticks; a small steady fire which didn't dry my dress and my pants, which he called my drawers, but which was very beautiful and smelled lovely. We sat by it for about twenty minutes, then it went out and we sat by the embers for another half-hour.

Then we made love again and that seemed to reach a new dimension which I'm used to now, but wasn't then. And that night for the first time I loved the sea, every surging wave and dipping sail; every sleeping captain and forsaken merman, I loved tenderly like a brother.

We didn't start home until one. I was still dressed in the rug.

At the second set of lights we came to, a van drove right into us; a frightful smack which threw him against me and both of us nearly out of the car. For a time we couldn't believe that we both seemed to be unharmed. I kept feeling my teeth and my nose and his teeth and his nose and my chin and his chin. 'Are we all right?' we asked each other. We couldn't believe it.

We couldn't spend long, though, over these tender solicitations, before becoming aware of the van and its driver, and a man hurrying towards us from the side road. We sat up. He got out of the car and I pulled on my wet dress and threw the rug on to the back seat.

He and the man who had joined us, a waiter on his way

31

home from work, managed to release the driver who was conscious but very dazed and angry. Another man came out of a nearby house and told us he had phoned the police and ambulance.

He wandered back and said he'd get a mini-cab to take me home since he'd probably be delayed by the police. He sounded distant, like someone with no more change phoning from a kiosk.

'But what about you?'

'It doesn't matter about me. I wasn't going home, anyway. I'm off to Germany in the morning, I intended staying at Gatwick tonight.'

'Germany? How long will you be in Germany?'

'About a fortnight.'

'Oh.'

'However, I'll have to be back for some pressing business round about next Friday, so I'll be seeing you as usual.'

'Are you sure? From Germany? Are you sure?'

He didn't answer because the police had arrived.

They seemed nice. Although we were clearly blameless, I'd expected a measure of disapproval, but they seemed pleased to be with us, striding about with notebooks and purposeful expressions like television cops. One of them phoned the local cab firm on our behalf. The driver of the van, cursing rather a lot and saying he was already late home, was taken off to hospital and then the car arrived for me. He directed the driver, paid the fare and kissed me. He made me keep his jacket.

The cab driver was a small, pale, tired-looking man who kept giving me quick sideways looks as he drove. I was frightfully uncomfortable, the skirt of my dress was still wet, and the jacket, though I was very pleased to have it, didn't succeed in keeping me warm. After a while I took it off and put it over my knees and my legs.

'It's turned cold,' I said, because he was looking at me.

'What'll your husband say?' he asked.

'About what?' Had the policeman told him something or was he guessing?

'About what? About what you've been up to.'

I decided not to answer. He'd been paid to drive me home, not to censure my morals. I closed my eyes.

'I know what I'd do if I was your husband. I know what I'd do.'

I pretended not to hear. 'I know what I'd do, don't I just.' I was suddenly frightened, a high, frenzied note had got into his voice and the car swerved. Of course I wasn't at all surprised when he pulled up in a lay-by, I realized that I'd been expecting it since I first saw him.

Nothing can possibly happen to me, I told myself, I'm much bigger and stronger than he is. At worst, it's going to mean a long delay, nothing more than that. How unpleasant, though.

He was in a very excited state. 'You're naked, aren't you, under that bit of a dress.'

I felt in the pockets of the jacket that was over my knees and pulled out cigarettes and lighter. I lit a cigarette and offered him one.

He ignored me and started fumbling with his zip.

'Listen to me,' I said very quietly. 'My friend is an extremely powerful man and I can assure you that if you as much as lay a finger on me, you'll go to prison, I can absolutely assure you of that; it won't be for the first time, either, will it? Do you honestly think it's worth it – a scuffle in the car? Look at me, I'm pretty strong.

'Have a cigarette,' I said again. He hadn't moved towards me.

'Come on. Have a cigarette and pull yourself together. Do you think they'll let you keep your licence if I report this? And if you keep me here more than a couple of minutes, I'm going to report it. Honestly.' I lit another cigarette and passed it to him and, my God, he took it. He smoked about half, inhaling deeply, then wound down the window and threw away the other half and started up the car. He'd even thought I was serious about the time-limit. He drove off without addressing another remark to me.

I'd never in my life spoken so authoritatively. I'd hardly

33

recognized my voice. I'd sounded like someone else, and I suddenly realized who it was. 'If you keep me waiting more than a couple of minutes, I'm going to report it.' My games teacher at school: it had come directly from her.

I wanted to sit back and relax as we got nearer and nearer South London; I wasn't even cold any more; but I dared not. I kept looking straight in front of me with my games-teacher scowl. 'Teresa Hardiman, exert yourself. Keep your eye on the ball and go for it.'

Dear old Miss Buxton. Fancy you coming to my rescue tonight. I'm sorry now I made your life such a misery, dawdling in the changing-cubicles, giggling at the goal posts, refusing to enter into the spirit of it, having a painful period on every single House Match for three or four years. I'm sorry.

'You can't be as damned stupid as you pretend to be, Tessa Hardiman. It's not humanly possible.' Nothing is wasted, ever, not even hockey.

I thought of her all the way home. When he stopped outside the door, I tugged my wet skirt from the seat with as much dignity as I could, got out and said, 'Try not to be so damned stupid again. It's just not worth it.'

I unlocked the door and let myself in. It was gone three. I buried my face in the jacket for a minute before I hung it up, and smelt its warm, comforting smell. Then I cleaned my teeth and went to bed. John didn't wake.

I couldn't sleep. What was I about? I didn't regret what I was doing but I was amazed at it, above all amazed that I felt it was my right. Yet I'd never expected to be an unfaithful wife, it didn't seem to fit in with any of my past life. How little I understood myself. Wasn't my marriage important to me? Since when? Who else was I, apart from the me I thought I knew, and old Miss Buxton? Who else?

I tried to let my mind go blank while I drifted back to the beginning, to the earliest sensations: wetting the bed, warmth turning cold, my Christmas stocking rustling in the darkness; out in the night for the first time, stars so beautiful that I cried

34

and my mother said it was hunger; the first day at school, a scratchy new uniform and a lot of noise.

Junior school life so uneventful that nothing remains of it. Years of ordinary middle-class life, no violence or accident or separation to darken the canvas; my father didn't come home drunk, my mother didn't weep or leave home, no man offered me sweets and a ride in the car, I was never chased by a bull nor bitten by a dog nor even separated from my tonsils. I suppose it was a happy, carefree life but hopeless stuff for self-analysis. Years of nothing. Nothing.

I remember being sick at school because I had to read in assembly, when was that? I was in Miss Druce's class. I can remember how I looked when I was in Miss Druce's class. I wore a grey pinafore-dress and my hair in bunches. I was a monitor; my job to clean the blackboard and give out pens and atlases. I was thought bossy.

My name is Tessa Hardiman. I live at 17 Gold Acre Road. I am in class 4 in Bridgeton Primary School. My father works in Insurance and my mother is a housewife and also runs things like the Red Cross. I have one sister. Her name is Barbara Hardiman and she is in Hillbrook Grammar School. She is four years older than me and she is very clever. She is not like the sisters in the books I read.

Barbara has emerged. Oh, she was an influence all right. Good, clean, punctual, clever Barbara. She put things ready the night before. Her hair was never tangled or untidy because she brushed it night and morning. She rolled up her hair ribbons and never forgot her dinner money. She practised the piano when she came home from school and enjoyed doing her homework. Father's favourite. She *liked* going to church with him on Sundays.

As small children we played together because there was no one else available, but I could always sense her relief when it was my bedtime.

The general verdict was that she was the clever one, but I didn't envy her much at that time. She could rarely answer my questions. She, it seemed to me, liked to assimilate only those boring facts which would enable her to do well at

35

school; she used to let me test her when her exams were imminent and I could never fault her, she could always reel off what was written so neatly in all her exercise books; whereas what I wanted was complete and immediate enlightenment on certain things which happened to take my interest, though they might not have any bearing on my school work, indeed usually didn't. At first I simply thought we were different.

As I got older, though, and more conformist, I tended to accept that she was immensely clever and I rather stupid.

When I followed her to the grammar school, every teacher mentioned my brilliant sister. 'Barbara is a first-class student, I do hope you'll work like Barbara.' Of course I never did, not for years, anyway.

I'd never before thought so deeply about the two of us, had never realized what a shadow she cast. How immaculate she was, how admired. She looked wonderful even in the box-pleated gym slips we had to wear.

'Isn't your sister good-looking.' It was always good-looking, not pretty nor beautiful, but good-looking. She had a perfect oval face, you didn't notice any particular feature because they were all so perfectly proportioned, and she was the right height and the right shape. She became head prefect. She had a boyfriend, Peter, who was dark and handsome. Everyone said they made a lovely pair. They had a good, healthy relationship, they played a lot of tennis and jointly organized the church youth club.

I was taller; by Barbara's side, a large girl. My eyes were said to be beautiful but my nose was too long and my mouth too large. I wanted a boy-friend like perfect Peter, but he didn't materialize and I didn't go out much in case it would seem that I was over-anxious. When I was in the Sixth I did nothing but work, and though unsystematic and haphazard, some of it stuck. Because Barbara had won a major scholarship to Oxford, I desperately needed to get to some University, if only by the skin of my teeth. She was always ahead of me like a bloody beacon.

I started to laugh. In bed by John's side I was suddenly

convulsed by laughter. I couldn't stop. It was clear to me that I'd married my sister. John was good-looking too in precisely the same band-box way, and very clever, and he worked methodically and efficiently just like Barbara. But instead of ignoring me, John wanted me around. In responding to John, I was catching up with Barbara, attaining what I'd pursued for so long.

It seems far-fetched now, but then it seemed like the whole truth; it explained everything and was also very, very funny.

The sea and the brandy and the awful cabman had been too much for me, I couldn't stop laughing. As soon as I seemed to grow calmer, I started again.

Finally, of course, John woke up. 'Whatever's the matter with you?' he asked, and his voice sounded so hard and cold that I stopped immediately, realizing that it wasn't really funny, but rather tragic. Comedy and tragedy had never seemed so close as that night when I finally settled down to sleep.

Chapter 5

Summer suits me, it turns my mousey hair blonde and my sallow skin golden, even my eyes have more colour in them; but that summer there was something extra; I was blooming. Everyone noticed it. Workmen jostled each other, forgetting to whistle, the greengrocer absent-mindedly picked the best fruit for me from the front of the display shelves, the milkman leaned back on the door-post and muddled up the bill, and the other wives on the estate became catty. 'Lose a stone in weight, dear,' they said, 'and you could be a model.'

But I didn't want to be a model. I was perfectly happy as I was, his mistress, a fancy-woman, a sex kitten ('At sixteen she knew everything there was to know and then some') living for Friday evenings. That's all I wanted.

But nothing remains static, I should have realized it. On the Monday morning, three days after my unexpected meal at Ambleside Mill, as I was pushing Dora and Toby home for lunch (when I collected Dora from Nursery School she was usually so tired that she used to squeeze into the push-chair with Toby) a car pulled up and it was him; there he was and offering us a lift.

I started to refuse, thinking at first that he was in Bromley's Queen's Road on other business, but Dora was tired of Toby sitting on her hip and said, 'Oh *please*, Mummy, let's go home in the car, oh *please*.' And immediately he was out and helping me fold up the pushchair. Not wishing to mix business and pleasure, I sat with the children in the back.

'Would you like a milkshake?' he asked Dora.

'Oh yes, please.' Dora closed her pale blue eyes and fluttered her long eyelashes. I was glad that she looked so smart, even with poster paint down the front of her green smock she looked like little Miss Pears.

'Ice-cream?' he asked Toby, who buried his face in my neck and growled.

'Yes, please,' Dora translated. 'He simply loves ice-cream and so do I. Do I like ice-cream best, Mummy, or milkshake?'

I refused to help her with that problem, having plenty of my own. I found I was uneasy to be with him and the children on a Monday morning. Would the children eat their lunch after the large ice-creams and unwholesome-looking drinks he was buying them? How would I explain the incident? There was no point in hoping that Dora wouldn't mention it, it was clearly going to be the highlight of her social life for quite some time; the big car, the big man, the big café, the big ice-cream. Even Toby was now managing a few words and always the wrong ones.

'Nice children,' he said over their bent heads, and I smiled my agreement.

'You do translations, don't you?' he asked. He must have been talking to Carole again. I admitted it.

'Russian?'

'No, only French.'

'Could you do some work for me? Say, one or two mornings a week? I'm serious.'

'What sort of work? I don't think I could manage any technical stuff. Besides, I couldn't leave Toby.'

'Is he too young for Nursery School? He looks very competent.'

Toby had poured some of the frothy pink drink into his chocolate ice-cream and was half drinking, half sucking the mixture over the side of the silver dish with loud, happy noises.

'He's only just two.'

'Couldn't you get someone in to look after him? We'd pay you well. You're a graduate, aren't you? You should do something other than house-keeping and baby-minding.'

'I do do something other than house-keeping and baby-minding.'

We clutched each other's hands under the table.

'When could you start?'

'Start what?'

'The job I'm offering you.'

'When would you like me to start?'

'On Monday, September 12th. That's when Dora re-starts school.' (How had he found that out?)

To me, everything seems plain sailing when it's six weeks ahead. I felt sure I could get someone in to look after Toby.

'All right. September 12th.'

'Don't forget to put it in your diary.'

'I don't have a diary,' I said, 'I only have Fridays.'

I realized I shouldn't be admitting so much, so I looked up at him and squinted. But he didn't smile.

'There are only Fridays for me, too,' he said, 'and it's not enough. That's why I want Monday mornings as well.'

'It won't be the same.'

'No, not the same. But you can come in and have coffee with me, I'll have several things to discuss with you, I'll be able to wander in and look at you from time to time, we'll have lunch together and then I'll put you on the train home. It'll be something. Quite a lot. Can you come up on Wednesday afternoon for the interview?'

'What interview?'

'The interview for the job.'

'I don't want to be interviewed. Who'll be interviewing me, for God's sake?'

'I will.'

'Oh.'

'Don't you see, it'll put our relationship on a proper footing, it'll be natural for you to be around, I'll be able to ring you up.'

'But I'm not sure that I want our relationship to be on a proper footing.'

Dora had finished eating and drinking and was listening to us with a rapt expression.

'What is a footing?' she asked him. 'Is it Mummy having her foot on top of yours? Can I have a footing, please?' She put her foot on mine which was, indeed, on his, and we sat like that for a moment or two. Until Toby had made it clear that his dish was licked really clean and that there was nothing else worthy of his attention.

'Three o'clock, Wednesday afternoon,' he said.

'All right.' He probably knew that my mother-in-law was staying and would be able to baby-sit.

He drove us home.

After lunch I told my mother-in-law about the interview. I told her it was a wonderful opportunity that might lead to a well-paid full-time job when Dora and Toby were both at school.

As she folded her lips together I remembered that she didn't believe in mothers going out to work, so I added that I'd be able, naturally, to do most of the work at home. I reminded her that with my third-class degree I wouldn't be able to get a wonderful creative job like John's, so that I should, perhaps, jump at the offer of this particular translating job in order to supplement the family income so that we could buy a caravan and a piano; two things she believed in.

Of course, that was different, she had to agree, and she had no objection to looking after the children on Wednesday afternoon, and if I wanted to have my hair done in the morning, curled a bit, say, then she was quite prepared for that too.

John seemed quite pleased at the prospect of my working, though I could see he was rather surprised that I'd managed to get a job and amazed that I had remembered the date of Dora's new term and had worked out, in theory at least, what to do with Toby.

'What firm is it?'

I had to admit that I wasn't certain.

'It's Walt's firm,' I said. 'I'll go round tonight to get the address.'

'Oh, Walt fixed it for you,' he said. 'That explains it.'

It was more difficult to explain to Carole how I'd come by the job.

'I just bumped into him in Queen's Road,' I said. 'Well, how do I know what he was doing in Queen's Road? He just asked me whether I could do some translating for him. I thought it was you who must have told him about me; I came over to thank you.'

41

'I did talk to him about you, yes. Well, he asked after you. When we had a meal with them. Didn't I tell you about it? Last Tuesday. Oh, it was super.'

They'd been to dinner at his house, the boss's house, they and three other couples.

'It was all very simple,' was all she would say. Even the house; well, it was very big and the garden was big, but even the house was sort of simple, if I understood what she meant. The meal was good but not fantastic. Simple, I suggested, and she agreed with me. There was a woman helping at the table, quite an ordinary, elderly woman whom the wife had called Nanny, which was strange because they didn't have children.

'What was she like?' I asked.

'Oh, sort of fifty to sixty, quite ordinary, plumpish.'

'No, the wife.'

'Oh,' she said. 'You mean Elspeth. Oh, she's really charming, very intelligent and elegant, you can see he's very fond of her.'

Well, I'd asked for that.

Walt wasn't in, but Carole gave me the address and told me what bus I'd need from Charing Cross.

John's mother had come for her usual two weeks, the last two weeks of July, the time she and her husband had always taken their holiday when he was alive.

'Have you and John quarrelled?' she asked me the following night when we were washing up together. I was surprised at her directness, she's a reserved woman as a rule.

'No, nothing like that.'

'What, then?'

'Nothing like that.' The kitchen was filled with the sound of breathing.

'Ask him,' I said, when she'd wiped the last cup and was returning to her knitting in the sitting-room.

I stayed on in the kitchen, ironing.

I loved ironing at that time, saving it until the children were in bed so that there was no one I had to talk to or keep an eye on, and nothing to do but let the iron glide over the lovely drip-dry cottons and think sweet thoughts.

But after my mother-in-law's disturbing question, other thoughts intruded; worries about John.

How were things with him? I really didn't know. On Wednesdays he stayed on in Town, getting back on the last train, just before one. I was always in bed when he got home and we never seemed to talk. He certainly wasn't happy, the more I considered it, the more sure of that I became. If he had a girl-friend, she didn't seem to be doing him much good.

I was the only one to have benefited from the time-to-ourselves arrangement he'd proposed. He seemed, if anything, more angry and bitter than before.

I felt worried, and not only on his account. What if he were to decide that the experiment had been a failure and ask me to forgo my nights out? I couldn't and wouldn't, of course, but how to explain my refusal? Would I tell him everything; how things were with me? What if he demanded that I give up my affair, threatened to divorce me otherwise? Would I be prepared to sacrifice our eight-year-old relationship – a steady and tender relationship it had been for several years, it was still a caring one – for the crazy, physical, probably short-term affair I was having on the side? I was sure I would, but I felt pretty rotten about it. I ought to think of my children, they were my responsibility, I had wanted them more than he had.

When I went into the sitting-room after finishing the ironing, I found him alone.

'Where's your mother?'

'She went to bed.'

'At ten o'clock? Without saying good night? What happened?'

'I bit her head off.'

'Why?'

'She lectured me.'

'What about?'

'Christ, do you really want to know? It was very boring.'

'Yes.'

43

'About marriage and fidelity and responsibility. I told her I didn't care a fig for any of them.'

'Are you drunk?' I asked. Suddenly I felt tender and protective towards him.

'Probably.'

'Why are you drinking so much, John? Are you in trouble about something?'

'For God's sake, don't you start.'

'Wouldn't it help, though, to talk to someone?'

'You're the last person I could talk to.'

'Why? Try me.'

'Because you're my wife, that's why.'

'That seems a very old-fashioned idea. I thought ours was a modern marriage, going our own ways, and so on.'

'OK, OK, but I still couldn't talk about it. Don't ask me to.'

He poured me a drink and we watched the second part of 'News at Ten'. I tried hard to concentrate on it. I think we'd just won the World Cup or something of that sort, and I remember envying all the excited crowds that they were showing ('England! England!'); all the people who cared about it, *really* cared, so that their own little personal problems, their own shabby hopes and desires, were, for a time at least, quite obliterated. It seemed wonderful to me, as wonderful in a way, and quite as incomprehensible, as being able to forget oneself in religion.

The news finished, John switched off the television and went back to his desk.

'Why don't you come to bed; it would do you good. You stay down working every night; you really don't look well.'

It was true. I hadn't noticed how deep the shadows were under his eyes.

'I don't stay down working,' he said, his voice sounding strange and dry, 'I stay down hoping to get a phone call.'

How strange it is to hear one's husband confessing to an abject love for someone else. I felt jealous as hell, that was a strange thing, as well as alarmed for the future, about the prospect

44

of change when I was happy as I was. Most of all, though, it was tenderness I felt. He looked so like Dora, about to cry and make a scene. Oh, I was mixed up.

'Come to bed,' I said. 'Can't we try to straighten things out a bit?'

He shook his head. 'You're good to me, Tessa.'

'No, I'm not,' I said, willing him to understand a little of how things were with me.

I went up to bed alone.

Chapter 6

That night, again, I couldn't sleep. Perhaps I'd gone to bed too early.

I was nervous about the future. On the one hand I'd got more than I'd ever dreamed of, more than I knew existed in the world in spite of all the poetry I'd read, on the other hand my marriage was clearly in a parlous state. And I believed in marriage. I believed in the family.

It was fashionable, I knew, to regard it as a monster; its members destructively locked together (I was, even then, viewing a four-part serial on that theme; a mother's suicide, the intolerable family pressures which had led to it.)

What I'd witnessed in real life was the other side of the coin: a sixty-five-year-old woman battling to keep her cleaning job at the clinic in order to support her 'fallen' daughter and her baby; a rough, tough Irishman, a gardener at the local park, transformed to womanly tenderness by his grown-up son's almost fatal motor-bike accident. Extraordinary sacrifices and patient devotion was what I'd seen; perhaps we all find evidence of what we wish to believe.

Anyway, my background – middle-class, C. of E. – was too conventional for me to accept very easily the idea of a broken marriage and a divided family. Far down in me somewhere was a puritanical woman (lady?) who found something subversive and shabby about the very word 'divorce'; undertones of malicious whispers and poison-pen letters and seedy hotels.

The scandal of my mother's cousin Violet had cast quite a shadow on my childhood; behind the little I'd understood of it, the troubled mass I hadn't.

Violet had broken off her engagement to a most eligible but probably dull schoolmaster and married a Yankee soldier. I think I must have been about five at the time. My grandmother, who lived with us when my father was in the army, wouldn't attend her wedding nor send her the dozen silver tea-spoons she gave to all her nephews and nieces, but sent instead two pillow-slips with what she called 'machine embroidery' and 'gipsy lace'. I remember venturing the opinion that they were pretty; I can still recall the bright pink, blue and yellow flower sprays at each corner; and my grandmother saying, 'Violet won't think much of them. She'll understand.'

'But what did she do?' I asked my grandmother. 'She let her feelings run away with her.' I suppose she'd had to get married.

Violet went to America, her picture was in all the national papers, one of the first GI brides to cross the Atlantic; she wrote long letters to my mother saying what a wonderful time she was having, what a splendid house they had near a large park, a kitchen like in the movies and a convertible and a station-wagon (which I imagined like the trolley pushed by the porter at our local station and thought a strange thing to boast about); but my grandmother continued to think of her with scorn and I with pity. Indeed, in my memory Violet became, and still remains, indistinguishable from another cousin who died young.

I don't think anything worse happened in our family, though I often heard my grandmother hint at shameless goings-on in others. She was certainly a stickler for the rules. Her face, full of righteous anger, was suddenly before me : My mother had come home after seeing the Olivier film *Lady Hamilton* and was telling Barbara and me something of the story. 'And wasn't Lord Nelson a *married man* at the time,' my grandmother said, 'and aren't you ashamed to be mentioning that *hussy* to these innocent mites.' 'It's History,' my mother said, and to our relief carried right on, but my grandmother sailed out of the room, leaving behind her a palpable unease.

But surely I'd got over my grandmother's strictures by this time? After all, she'd been dead over fifteen years. Well, obviously I had. I'd embraced the position of hussy readily enough, I was half-way to being liberated. All the same . . . all the same, I was horrified at the thought that what I did in such light-hearted and delicious fashion could conceivably affect the lives of my children. And if I wasn't careful, it

47

surely would. If John was behaving irresponsibly, there was all the more reason why I should be employing my energies in trying to save the marriage. Because if John and I split up, how could I be sure that the children would be as happy and secure as if we stayed together? That's roughly what my thinking that night amounted to. With a little extra pain on my own account; I still had affection for John and considered him mine; old-fashioned thinking, old-fashioned possessiveness.

I couldn't sleep. John came to bed – I don't think he'd had a phone call – and a short time afterwards a bird began to sing. I sat up in bed thinking it must be a Bromley nightingale, only to realize that it was the first blackbird welcoming another day. It was four-fifteen. In the greyish half-light I could just make out John's profile. By the time the dawn chorus had faded out, I could see him clearly, his rather severe good looks; even asleep he looked tormented.

I decided to cancel my interview and to concentrate on trying to save my marriage, though I wasn't at all sure how to go about it. I slept then until Toby woke me at half past seven.

Breakfast was an even quieter meal than usual that morning, John and his mother passing each other things that neither wanted, and only the children talking. John left for work. An hour later I took Dora to school.

When the post came I opened the only letter, a rate demand, and told my mother-in-law that my interview had been postponed.

As soon as she'd left the house, bound for the park with Toby and a bag of crusts, I telephoned his firm.

I asked for his secretary. I asked her to give him a message, Mrs Jilks regretted, etc. I put the phone down. I was trembling.

I wanted to see him. I wanted to be interviewed. I wanted to see his secretary, his office, the people that worked for him. Perhaps he'd have told me something about himself, his aims and ambitions; I knew so little about him. Afterwards I'd have been able to imagine him at his desk. Why was that suddenly so important, what his desk was like, even the wall and the window behind it, his chair, his telephone? What was I hoping to achieve by denying myself the pleasure of his company for that short, summer afternoon? What was it going to lead to? Was I going to refrain from going out with him next Friday evening? If not that, why this?

When the telephone rang an hour or so later I thought it would be him, I thought I had the chance to revoke my too-hasty decision, but it was John.

'I rang to say that I won't be staying out tonight,' he said. 'I thought I'd better let you know that I'll be home for dinner.'

'I see.'

'You don't seem very pleased.'

'I am pleased.'

'Why?'

'Why? I'm not sure. I suppose I'm hoping it's a sign that things may improve a bit between us.'

'What do you do when you go out on Friday nights?'

'I meet a man.'

'You're a bloody quick worker!'

'Yes.'

'You meet a man!'

'Wasn't that what you intended? Something along those lines?'

'I hadn't considered what you'd do.'

'Does it upset you?'

'Yes, it does. The irony of it upsets me.'

'John, if you asked me to give him up, I would.'

There was a long pause. I was very frightened.

'I don't think I can. There's someone I can't give up.'

'Even though it's not bringing you any happiness or peace or fulfilment?'

'Even though, as you say, it's not bringing me any happiness or peace or fulfilment.'

'Let's go out together on Friday night.'

'Where?'

'To a concert at the Festival Hall. Like we used to.'

'I don't know. That doesn't seem fair on you.'

'But you're coming home tonight, you're making a gesture. Think about it, anyway. It would please your mother.'

'All right, I'll think about it. Thank you.'

'I'll see you later, then.'

'Fine.'

I sat down heavily on the settee in the sitting-room. Why was I such a cowardly and conventional hypocrite? What if John took me up on my offer ('If you asked me to give him up, I would')? How could I even think of giving him up when his presence filled me with such happiness? As I dried my eyes and blew my nose and got ready to meet Dora from nursery school, something struck me with revelationary force. I loved him. I loved him. Oh my God, I loved him.

It made everything so much more dangerous.

At this point, I must clear up an obscurity. So far, I've never given him a name. The reason is that at the beginning I thought his name, Victor, old-fashioned and pompous; unlike him and unworthy of him.

Walt had always called him Fielding, which I thought quite distinguished; I was saddened when I discovered his first name, I thought it so terribly unromantic. I don't mean that I needed him to have a name like Tristan or StJohn; any Tom, Dick or Harry would have done, or Michael or Paul or even Geoffrey, but I couldn't take Victor to my heart, so I never called him anything.

It may be a trivial and inconsequential thing to report, but in that moment when I realized I loved him, I found myself saying, 'Victor, Victor, Victor,' and it sounded tender, passionate and celebratory. Oh Victor, Victor, Victor.

The year, as I mentioned, is 1966, the middle of the frenzied, brutal, confused decade. And I, having discovered a great love, am now intent on sacrificing it to save, if I can, a dry and sterile marriage.

'Is The Man coming today?' Dora asked as I met her.

'No, not today.'

'Will he come tomorrow?'

'I don't think so. Not tomorrow.'

'If not tomorrow, it's Sometime Soon, isn't it, Mummy?'

John came home as he'd promised. He had a game with Toby and carried him to bed. He read to Dora. We had dinner. He was attentive to his mother and to me. He cleared the table and offered to wash up. His mother and I washed up and afterwards he and I played a game of chess while she knitted. At half past nine, his mother suggested that we should go out to have a drink since we had her to baby-sit, but I insisted that he take her out; he could take me any old time, I said.

They went out. And as the front door closed behind them, with all the precision of French farce the telephone rang and it was him: Victor.

'Tessa, what happened? Can you talk?'

'Yes.'

'What happened? Why didn't you come this afternoon?'

'I decided that I mustn't complicate my life any further. I mustn't come on Friday either.'

'Of course you must. You must.'

'Why?'

'Because we need each other.'

'Need?'

'Yes, need. Need. It's very simple.'

'I don't want to talk about it.'

'Tess, please come on Friday. I'll be waiting for you. I'll be in the Falcon till closing time. Don't let me down, Tess.'

'Please don't wait for me. I've made the decision. It's very difficult for me.'

'Why is it difficult for you?'

'Don't ask me.'

'Why is it difficult for you?'

'Good night, Victor.'

I put the phone down and went upstairs and ran a bath.

I couldn't even cry. I felt utterly exhausted as though I'd cried for hours and hours.

That night was bad enough, but it wasn't anything like as dreadful as the Friday evening when John and I went to a concert at the Festival Hall; every minute was a tearing agony. I kept on being tempted to rush out and take a taxi to Bromley to see whether he was still at the Falcon.

Why didn't I take note of how I felt? That night for the first time I felt I was being unfaithful.

The following week dragged by. Every time the telephone rang I was on tenterhooks, but he didn't ring again. It was fortunate that my mother-in-law was still with us so that at least I was occupied in entertaining her, arranging outings and so on.

One day we went to Whipsnade Zoo; I think it was a Saturday, the last day of her visit. I still recall that day as one of the bleakest of my life. As always, it was windy and cold on the Downs, every animal looking as though it would like to be snug and cosy behind bars.

My mother-in-law remembered (and recounted in interminable detail) the previous time she'd been there while her husband was alive.

'Do you remember, John, we'd brought a picnic with us, egg and cress sandwiches probably, that was his favourite, and two flasks of tea, he was a one for his cup of tea. Do you remember how long we had to stop at the lion enclosures, he liked the big cats, didn't he, John, and I remember there were two little girls, about six and seven, who kept following us about because he'd started giving them fruit pastilles – he always carried pastilles because of his chest – and whenever we stopped to look round, they'd laugh and run back to their mum and dad. He was very fond of kiddies, wasn't he, John? What a shame he never saw these two; he'd have spoiled them dreadfully, he could never say no to kiddies.'

Her mournful reminiscences accompanied us through the chill, windy afternoon. Toby was teething and wouldn't take an interest in anything and Dora kept whining to go on the train and John was walking about like a man in a dream.

As I bathed the children that night, I remember hugging them; holding them, wriggling and living and plump in my arms. They were all I had.

Chapter 7

Within a couple of weeks it was our holiday; we were spending a fortnight in a small hotel in Devon.

During the first week, the weather was poor but not hopeless. We went for pleasant walks along the cliffs and Dora and Toby were able to have an hour or two on the sand every day, even if occasionally in anoraks and wellingtons.

One day seemed destined to be rather fraught; Toby swallowed a pebble and Dora got her fingers stuck in a PDSA collecting box within minutes of reaching the beach; and it went on that way, but by and large there was nothing worse than the usual lost sandals, beach balls carried out to sea and ice-cream tummy-ache.

The hotel was comfortable and the food good. The children were tolerated and provided with high-tea, though no one went as far as asking what they wanted, let alone patting them on the head and smiling.

When they went to bed, Toby sleeping wonderfully as a result of wind and spray, we had a peaceful dinner and afterwards read or played Scrabble or looked at television. One night we ate out with another couple in a restaurant overlooking the sea.

At the beginning of the second week, the weather changed. For sixteen hours a day the sun shone from cloudless skies and the temperature reached the eighties. By mid-day the children were bored by the sand and sea. Dora's shoulders burned in spite of all the lotion I put on them. (How well I remember her sweet, thin, quivering shoulder blades.)

John found a small park, green and shady, at the other end of the village and took the children there for an hour or so after lunch, leaving me to enjoy the sun.

As soon as they were out of sight, I used to take off my sunglasses and shut my book and indulge in a juvenile bout of day-dreaming which took the form of Victor's arriving by helicopter or small boat and our reunion. So sharp was my desire for him on one occasion that I actually left my deck-chair and walked round the headland and up the cliff to find the isolated spot I'd take him to when he came.

I found a grassy hollow hidden from everyone, and I stood in it squinting up at the seagulls and the bright blue sky.

'By gum,' somebody said, and a man stood up from an adjoining hollow.

'I only shut my eyes for half a minute,' the man said, 'and here she is.' He was tall and handsome, fair hair, a wonderful drooping moustache and a tan as shiny as mine. He came over to the edge of my hollow and sat on a stone, looking at me.

'You're staying at the Gresham, aren't you?' he said. He had a friendly smile and very broad shoulders.

'Yes. Are you?'

'No. I'm a local. Well, sort of. I've got the caravan park and the pleasure boat.'

'I was looking for a nice picnic spot,' I said. It seemed necessary to say something, if only to break his concentration.

'Were you?'

'I thought I'd bring the kids up here later on.'

'And I thought you seemed more like someone on the look-out for a nice chap like me. Wishful-thinking again. You don't look like anybody's mum.'

'I've got two children.'

'I know. I've seen them, boy and girl. Your husband's got them this afternoon?'

'Yes, he's taken them to the park. My little girl gets burned on the beach.'

'Does he take them every afternoon?'

'When it's hot.'

'What are you going to do, then, till they come back? Do you fancy staying here for a while?'

'No, I think I'll go back to my book now that I've found this place. It's not private or anything, is it?'

'It's not private property, no. But it's lovely and quiet.'

'Gosh, yes.'

'You don't feel like staying for a bit of a sunbathe now that

55

you've climbed all this way? You're not nervous or anything, are you? I mean, I'm very nice.'

'No, of course not.' I sidled away.

'My name's Bill, by the way, Bill Clarke.'

'I'm Tessa Jilks.'

'Tessa! That's a nice name. My grandfather had a sheep-dog called Tessa.'

He put two fingers in his mouth and whistled. He turned to face the brow of the hill and whistled several different notes, and stood, shading his eyes and scanning the hills as though expecting the imminent arrival of a large flock of sheep. It was an attractive display.

He seemed absorbed so I moved back a step or two towards the path.

'If you feel like coming up any afternoon,' he said, spinning round, 'I'm usually here round about this time.'

'I think I've given you the wrong impression,' I said, trying to sound haughty, but sounding nervous instead.

'I assure you, you haven't.'

'Well, goodbye then,' I said, and started to walk quite fast through the coarse sea grass back towards the beach.

' 'Bye, Tessa.' He whistled again and I turned round. He was waving.

I waved back.

As soon as I'd got back to my deck-chair and my boring paper-back I wished I'd stayed up there with him, flirting a bit, engaging in a slightly dangerous conversation. I put on my dress and went to the park to find John and the children.

But I couldn't put the encounter out of my head. When we were sitting in the lounge after dinner I went over it, word by word, glance by glance. I began to wonder about his thick moustache; what it would be like on my mouth. I'd never kissed a man with a moustache.

I wondered what he'd thought of me. Could he be imagining that I'd seen him go on to the cliffs and was following him? He probably could. 'A bloody nymphomaniac came after me today,' he'd probably be telling his pals in the Blue

56

Anchor. (I shouldn't mind slipping over to the Blue Anchor later on to see if he'd be there. I'd wash my hair and put on my black dress and drink beer with him and flirt with his pals.)

I was behaving like an adolescent, I realized it, bowled over by a man's admiration and smooth talk.

My only excuse was that I'd never had any admiration when I was an adolescent. For instance, I used to consider myself too fat to lie on the beach sunbathing, I used to rush out of the sea and into my clothes, cringing if anyone looked at me. Only Barbara, lean and lithe, got the glances. Being slim seemed the vital thing for the twentieth-century girl, like being virtuous and charitable in the Middle Ages. And not being slim, I never had the confidence to compete. I was never around. I never had a boy-friend till I met John.

In the Fifth, there were boys who took me home from school dances and other social functions, but in the Sixth I hadn't really done anything but work. As I've already mentioned, having a brilliant older sister kept me up to scratch. I simply had to get my A-levels; I was too busy to go out. And it was a wonderful excuse because I was too nervous to go out anyway.

When I met John in my first year at University – I was eighteen – I already regarded myself as on the shelf. I suppose that's why I never had a single doubt about his being right for me. We got engaged in my first year.

I found myself wishing that I could blame my background, my family, anything or anyone but myself for what I was beginning to realize was a very grave mistake. But I'd always felt secure and loved as a child, not even stifled or over-protected.

I was the younger daughter of contented and kind middle-class parents. My father was now an official of the National Farmers' Union. He liked farms and farmers and country ways. His father had been a vicar and he continued to go to church twice on Sundays as he had done as a boy. He watched television, especially anything to do with the war, read detective books and enjoyed company.

My mother and he seldom did anything together, yet there

seemed great amiability between them. She was constantly amused by him. 'Guess what your father's been up to?' she used to ask, as though he was no end of a fellow, and when we failed to guess, would chuckle and relate something so entirely unremarkable that we couldn't even smile. 'Oh, well, you wouldn't understand,' she'd say, as though hinting at some depths of depravity which only she could plumb.

She was probably the more important influence on my life. Within conventional limits, she was unconventional and carefree. Her life was a hurly-burly of constant activity, there was hardly anything going on in the small town where we lived that she didn't help run. I remember times when our breakfast room would be full of jumble for the Red Cross, the dining-room overflowing with a committee meeting for War on Want, and the sitting-room tawny with nervous Brownies waiting to be tested for badges. 'Tessa, love, have you got a moment, these clever girls want to tell you what they've learnt.' ('Give them all Grade 1, love, it encourages them.')

She was an erratic cook. 'She can't even cook a potato,' my father used to say sadly every Sunday lunchtime, and she used to beam her agreement. Yet it never deterred her from entertaining, and sometimes when she could muster enough helping hands in the kitchen the meal was a triumph. The greatest hazards were the long, long telephone conversations she used to have when other women made do with a quick sherry. 'Now, my dears,' she used to say, returning to the kitchen, 'what have we done so far?' Her Christmas cakes and puddings were always superb; she used to say that all the chopping and stirring relaxed her.

The great thing about my mother was that she never gave up anything for us. She carried on with her full and varied life and we had to like it or lump it. She didn't do too much for us, either. She worked her fingers to the bone quite often, but it wasn't for us, but only for much more deserving children.

Barbara and I used to be invited to friends whose mothers had spent hours over the tiny sandwiches and the home-made sausage rolls and cheese straws and four kinds of cake. Of

58

course, Mother allowed us to invite those friends to our house but we'd often find that she had to be elsewhere on the day. 'Have a wonderful time,' she used to say as she passed us on the doorstep. 'Why don't you have potatoes in their jackets with lots of butter, and tinned peaches afterwards? Would that be a good idea?'

One of my best friends was a girl called Brenda Tilson and I used to spend a great deal of time at her home. She lived in a flat over a shop. Her parents were much younger than mine (she once told me that her father was madly jealous of her mother and used to knock her about if she talked too long with any of the tradesmen. I was always in dread and hope that it would happen while I was there, but it never did). I thought her mother was rather shapeless and that she dyed her hair, but Brenda assured me that she had a perfect figure and didn't. I was impressed by her loyalty to her mother; I was always so quick to spot all the faults and failings of mine. Yet now, when people talk about the tensions which build up in families, I think of Brenda and her mother. Once I overheard a ferocious quarrel between them. 'And I gave you all the money I'd saved for my Hoover,' her mother was screaming, 'so that you could get that wretched bike.' (Brenda had a wonderful golden bike with three-speed and extraordinary handlebars.) I was only about fourteen at the time, but I remember feeling relieved that my mother would never, never sacrifice anything for me. A new Hoover she might give up; Mrs Mann and her daughters did most of the Hoovering anyway; but only for the RSPCA or the Lifeboat Institution. She would always be able to get me a very good bike from one of her jumble sales (she was proud that the huge black upright I had, had once belonged to a Rear-Admiral's wife. 'And you can be sure, she'd have got the very best.')

I have nothing at all against my parents. I seemed to have made a mess of my life quite unaided. What was there to explain why I should have rushed into marriage with the first, indeed the only man, who asked me? (I can't remember whether even he asked me, I think we simply gravitated

59

towards marriage almost as a consequence of spending so much time together in the library and lecture rooms and getting on so well.)

I'd been an idiot, that's all there was to it. The cold realization frightened me. I jumped up and said, 'Come on, let's go out to the Blue Anchor before they close,' and John looked at his watch and then at me, put down his book and said, 'Yes, all right.'

There was only one pub, and it was so full that most of the drinkers were out in the front, some at tables in the little garden, some sitting on the wall and some standing about in groups on the pavement outside. It was very pretty; lights in the trees, and the sea and the sky a soft violet-blue like the eyes of a new baby.

I wanted to go inside, that's where the locals would be, I felt sure, so we fought our way to the saloon bar. Two other people from our hotel, the couple we'd had dinner with the previous week, were sitting at a table near the window, and by the time John had managed to get our drinks they'd waved to tell us that there was room for us there. That wasn't what I'd wanted, but I had no option but to follow John and join them.

Anyway, I managed to look round before I sat, and saw Bill Clarke playing darts through in the other bar. My heart began to beat quite violently as he nodded at me and smiled. I sat down.

The couple we were with were scientific advisers to the Ministry of Agriculture and Fisheries. During our dinner together the previous week they'd been describing some of the experiments they were engaged on, and immediately we were seated they went on where they'd left off. John enjoys accumulating information of all sorts. If a cultured man is one whose mind touches life at the greatest number of places, then John is by definition cultured. He's interested in sport and politics and music and art and drama and philosophy and philology and archaeology and anthropology and folk-dancing and cross-word puzzles and calligraphy and stamps and butterflies and fossils and agriculture and fisheries, whereas my interests are fewer and more intense.

Luckily I could just see the dart players from where I was sitting, and after a bit I got to my feet as though completely enthralled by the game.

I had a nodding acquaintance with one other of the players; her son, a large, brutal five-year-old called Angus, had bashed down all Dora's beautiful sandcastles the previous morning; and when she saw me watching, she beckoned me over, she was waving three darts about in her other hand, and I made my escape. 'Shan't be a minute,' I said brightly.

'Hallo, Beautiful,' Bill mouthed as I joined them. He had his arm round a small, dark-haired girl dressed in pink whom he introduced as his wife.

'This is the lady I was telling you about,' he told her. 'The one that wants to see over the caravans.'

'Oh yes,' she said. 'When would you like to come up?'

Angus's mother had not acquitted herself too well at the board and her husband, an even larger and grosser version of Angus, was teasing her about it in an insensitive, beery way. 'Come to think of it, what can she do, har, har,' he was saying. 'One, she can make a pot of tea, two . . .' The list was drowned by a gust of ribald laughter.

'Tomorrow morning suit you?' Bill asked.

'Could I bring the children?'

' 'Course you can. There's a sand-pit and swings.'

'Perhaps you'd like a cup of coffee,' his wife said. 'We're in the bungalow at the top of the site.'

'Thank you.'

'It's your turn, Sue.' Bill gave his wife a little tap on the bottom, and as soon as she'd left turned all his attention to me.

'I don't want to see over any caravans,' I said, trying to speak crossly and longing for a little tap on the bottom too.

'Of course you do. They're very modern and the site is the prettiest in the West. That's what we've got on our brochures, anyway, though to be honest, scenery doesn't mean much to me. It wouldn't cost you a quarter of what you pay at the

Gresham. We open at Easter. We're already taking bookings for next Easter. Say the word and I'll reserve you the newest we've got; bath and shower, Calor gas and of course plumbing laid on.'

He was looking at me with some passion while coolly enumerating the mod. cons. His tan wasn't an even colour like mine but consisted of large, moist-looking freckles running into one another. His nose was very long and thin. His moustache looked quite silky, it had a slightly reddish tint in the artificial light, I wanted to touch it.

'I've got to go now. My turn.' He took the darts from his wife. I edged nearer to watch him play.

In about five minutes it was closing time and in about ten, people began to disperse. I slipped out through a side door hoping to miss John and find Bill somewhere in the warm night. I stood under a lamp.

He found me of course.

'I had to say that about the caravans,' he said, pulling me out of the light. 'She's jealous as hell; she'd think I was after you or something.'

'And you're not?'

' 'Course not, I've just brought you a brochure.'

He'd taken me to the side of the pub where it was dark. He lowered his beautiful moustache on to my lips but I suddenly pulled away.

'What's up?'

'My husband's there.'

'Where? There's no one there. Relax. Be nice.'

He pulled me to him again but I pushed him away with all my strength. I couldn't bear his touch. Everything about him was horrible. I pushed him away really hard so that he stumbled and almost fell. 'What the bloody hell's wrong with you? For the last half-hour you've been giving me the eye. What's bloody happened?'

'I've got to go,' I said, and ran up the hill until I overtook John and Roger and Tina Warrington, Agriculture and Fisheries, who'd decided not to wait for me.

I was crying, but in the dark they thought I was just out of breath. I wanted Victor, that's all, only Victor. At least I was glad to get it straight.

That night, John and I made love for the first time for months. I was nervous and awkward about it, feeling that he was performing a duty; that he'd noticed my tension and was ascribing it to the wrong cause. Several times I'd felt that I could be at least very tender and maternal towards him if he gave me the chance, but when he did, I was neither. We lay and sweated together for a time and broke away from each other still as separate as when we began. I didn't hate his touch as I'd hated Bill Clarke's, but that's about as much as I could say. We were much closer when we read Sartre together or played chess.

Chapter 8

Two days later we travelled home.

I've spent a long time wondering whether or not to fill in some details. I don't mean details of the landscape, descriptive passages, though travelling from the West Country to the outskirts of London on an August Saturday gives one plenty of time to observe the slowly shifting scene, almost to see the corn ripening. The details I can't decide about concern Toby's car-sickness. Mothers of children in the pre-school years might find it comforting to read of someone who suffered more or less, and I'm fairly sure it was more, than their Jason or Miranda, but I'm wondering how fair it would be on other women; let alone men; the childless, say, or those pregnant for the first time. I've decided to compromise by recording the facts starkly. He was sick seven times, once down my back and six times down my front, and Dora, a very nice girl but not a saint, whined through the six or seven hours because of the smell. Apart from that, it was an uneventful journey.

When we got back, Dora got her doll's pram from the garage and went off to see her friends at No. 7, Toby and I had a bath together and John carried things in from the car, from time to time calling out bits of information I could have done without: 'No letters', 'The milkman's only left one pint of milk', 'There's a dreadful smell in the kitchen.'

I was drying Toby when he came to the door of the bathroom to announce that we'd had a burglary. I went with him to the bedroom, carrying Toby in a towel.

Every article of clothing that we possessed had been left in a pile in the middle of the room, all the drawers wide open and empty. The wardrobes were ransacked, nothing left hanging. My jewel box had been searched, it was open and the contents left on the top of the dressing-table. (I'd taken my gold chain with me, I had very little else of any value.)

'They've taken my transistor,' John said. It was a new one,

olive green, his mother had bought it for his last birthday.

Toby was sitting in the middle of the pile of clothes, throwing things about, happy to be home.

'They don't seem to have taken anything of mine. What a nerve. It's not rubbish, you know. This brooch was my grandmother's.' I was trying to cheer John up, he seemed stricken.

'I can't take it in. Isn't it horrifying, to think they were here, in this room, turning over our things, handling our things, pricing them. All we have now is what they've rejected. Our things are polluted.' (He's much more imaginative than I am.) 'I'd better phone the police.'

He rushed up again. 'They've taken the silver frame from the dining-room.'

While he was phoning I started to get dressed, just picking things up at random from the pile on the floor, things I'd completely forgotten about.

I fetched things for Toby and started to dress him. Both his room and Dora's seemed quite untouched.

'They're coming straight away,' John said. 'At least that's what they said.'

'Guess what, I think Toby's got chicken pox.'

'Oh God, we seem to be cursed. Oh God.'

When Dora came in she counted all her dolls, furry animals, china horses, books, handbags, handkerchiefs, slides, hair ribbons, perfume bottles, crayons and pencils.

'They haven't taken anything of mine,' she was able to tell the policemen when they came. 'My red shoulder-bag was stolen once, but it was Debbie Lawrence done that.'

John announced that he was going to bed while I was still watching the chat show on television. 'What a tough customer you are,' he said. 'Toby's been sick all over his bed and he'll probably wake again soon and we've had this ghastly burglary and you just sit there, completely absorbed in that rubbish.'

'I'll be up soon,' I said.

When I heard him on the stairs, I got out my postcard again. It was from Victor. A view of the Acropolis. 'Work

65

piling up. Look forward to seeing you 12th September, *earlier if possible*. V.F.'

John must have seen it and dismissed it along with the bills and circulars and soap coupons as 'no letters', but how much it meant to me, that innocuous message, giving me another chance, and three weeks to decide whether or not to take it.

I studied the handwriting, every separate letter. I'd only seen his writing before on a cheque, it was like him, straightforward and direct (but I mustn't pretend to be a graphologist because it seemed to me sexy and tough and loving and gentle as well). I heard his voice, he repeated the words over and over, each time making it more urgently necessary for me to go to him. The simple message took on the force of the most passionate declaration. (Dearest Girl. The time is past when I had power to advise and warn you against the unpromising morning of my life.) How had I imagined that I could give him up when the truth was that I loved and desired him. I could almost feel his arms round me.

When I said that all our evenings together (seven) were entirely given over to sex, I was of course exaggerating. There were long spells when we lay on the tartan rug talking and holding hands. (There were times, too, when he'd lick my face all over, little tiny licks, he'd lick off all my eyeshadow and the thick, greasy stuff I put on my eyelashes, and though I didn't like it too much, I knew I'd never get him to stop until he wanted to, so I used to submit to it. 'You're like a mother cat,' I used to say when he'd finished. 'Yes, I am, aren't I?') He'd tell me about his childhood in Poplar, about being taken to the gasworks when he had whooping-cough, about seeing his grandfather in his coffin, about having a penny to go to the barber, twopence to go to the pictures, what sweets they had in the corner shop; tiger nuts and sweet tobacco; about the barrage balloons and the Blitz, about the time he was evacuated to Oxfordshire, the woman who'd bought him his first pair of pyjamas, the daughter he'd fallen in love with, the day his mother – and three aunties – had come to fetch him home, the doodle bugs. And I told him about the

66

awful books about dying children my grandmother used to read to us, and my father coming home from the army, and Barbara breaking my doll because she'd had an aeroplane, and about being ashamed of my mother's New Look.

I wanted to hear about the rest of his life. He hadn't told me anything after his return to Poplar when he was thirteen. How had he become so successful, a dynamic young executive Walt called him, though he wasn't so young, thirty-eight, which I then considered middle-aged. I had so much to find out.

Wasn't I giving up too much? What would be the point of keeping the family intact if I, its corner-stone, should become bitter and self-pitying? I almost managed to convince myself that it was my plain duty to resume the affair for the sake of the children; they wouldn't want me throwing crockery about and crying and committing suicide like the woman in the television serial.

Of course, people get over the most shattering love-affairs.

My sister, Barbara, for instance. She fell in love with a Frenchman whose children she was teaching during her pre-Honours year abroad. She was twenty-one – and I seventeen – at the time.

We had a letter from her just before she was due back, in which she invited me to go up to London to meet her; we'd stay there for a weekend before coming home; she'd earned a lot of money, she'd take me to the theatre, would like my company to go shopping, etc.

I was absolutely bowled over because we'd never been at all close. 'What's got into her?' I kept asking my mother, and she was as perplexed as I, though my father thought it very natural, very pleasant, absence making the heart grow fonder, two sisters, the closest companions, the best of friends.

I went, even though I hated shopping, which was one of her passions.

I remember meeting the boat train at Victoria and vainly trying to get used to the idea of a new relationship. After all, why shouldn't Barbara and I talk together? Other sisters did.

They lay in adjoining beds and talked long into the night, about boy-friends and books and religion.

The train was an hour late and I sat on a bench nervously considering topics of conversation.

We'd got a stupid young teacher for English at that time who was always trying to get us to have discussions when all we wanted to do was carry on with our work (luckily she only took us for two lessons a week), and it was noticeable that food was the only topic which elicited a fairly good response. Most of the form were willing to describe the scratch meal they'd prepare if their mothers were suddenly called away, whereas if she ever gave us a larger subject, what we hoped from life, for instance, or the true end of education, an awesome hush would descend.

OK, I'd stick to food. What sort of food did you have in France? I'd ask. I was so thrilled by the happy inspiration that I could hardly refrain from making a note of it. Was everything too oily? Do they really use as much garlic as Dad says? I was confident that she'd carry on happily on the subject, because she was fond of cooking and extremely fond of eating. 'Do you remember the description of the lunch at Oxbridge in Virginia Woolf's *A Room of One's Own*?' I could throw in quite casually when her descriptions of French meals flagged. (If she didn't, I could refresh her memory, having just read it on the train up.) Meals in books. Was this the sort of subject I ought to be aiming at? It seemed rather ambitious when our usual exchange was on the lines of 'Can I borrow your Chaucer?' 'Put it back when you've finished with it' or 'Are you going out tonight?' 'Yes.'

I was beginning to wish I hadn't come.

I went on to the platform and she was one of the last off the train. She looked absolutely stunning, I was almost glad to see her. She had on a putty-coloured suit in some wonderful, obviously French material that didn't crease, and a black blouse and two matching suitcases and dark glasses. She looked so disdainfully at some poor man who offered to help her that he almost melted on the spot. I felt proud to be approaching her so confidently.

'Oh, Tessa,' she said. 'I'm glad you were able to come.'

I took one of her suitcases (my shabby bag plus the inevitable paper carrier was in a locker) and we walked along the platform together.

'Tessa, I'm afraid I'm just making use of you,' she said.

I let that sink in. Was I, then, to be a kind of chaperon in some dangerous weekend adventure? On the whole, I was rather relieved. Nothing, I thought, would be as difficult as sudden intimacy with a distant and very superior sister. I asked no questions. I wasn't in any hurry for details.

'I've got to have an abortion,' she told me in the taxi. 'For God's sake don't be upset,' she said a moment later. My face must have given me away. I composed it.

'It's all been arranged. It will be completely straightforward. All I have to do is to go to a certain address by ten o'clock tomorrow morning, and at three o'clock the next day I'll be ready to leave. We'll go home on Sunday afternoon.'

The taxi dropped us at the small hotel in Russell Square where we'd always stayed with my parents. I'd never wanted them so badly.

We went up in the lift.

'I hope you don't mind sharing,' she said. 'I told him to get us the one room.'

I was moved. It was a much bigger room, probably more expensive, than the one we usually had; it had a wash-basin and fitted carpets and a couple of armchairs.

She tipped the porter and went to wash her hands. She took off her sun-glasses and looked at herself in the mirror.

'We'll go to the theatre tonight.'

'Oh, please, don't bother to do anything on my account.' I realized it was the first thing I'd said. I thought about the questions I'd prepared, and almost smiled.

'He booked seats for us, some bloody musical; he thought we'd want something light.'

She took out the tickets from her beautiful new handbag and passed them to me. They were a pound each, which was terribly expensive at that time.

'Let's try and get the money back,' I said. 'It's only four o'clock.'

'Tessa, you're a genius.'

It was a very popular musical and we got the money back without any difficulty. Then we went to the Old Vic and got tickets for *King Lear* at five-and-sixpence each. She also insisted on booking me a ticket for the next night (I was rather pleased that she was so sure I'd want to see it again the following night).

'I don't think I'll be able to bear to see it tomorrow,' I told her in the interval. 'Oh, don't be so stupid, I'm not having my eyes out.' We were getting on quite well.

I went with her to the nursing home, a dreadful grey London building like insurance offices, next morning. She kissed me swiftly on each cheek when the woman at the reception desk took her away. (She had told me in a most brisk and business-like way the previous night that the 'he' in question was of course her employer, but had offered no further details.) I went to the Tate in the afternoon and cried over several of the pictures, and to the Old Vic again in the evening where I cried from the opening curtain and went on so loudly and steadily that the woman next to me leaned over and asked me to stop. I was proud of Barbara, she was so brave.

The next afternoon, as instructed, I took a taxi to fetch her. My relief at seeing her waiting for me in the foyer on the third floor was indescribable; I'd spent all night preparing for the worst. Her face was a terrible colour under the tan, all her beauty had been knocked out of her, she looked like someone resurrected from the dead. She let me carry her small overnight bag.

'Put your glasses on,' I said. I couldn't bear to see how ill she looked.

We went down in the lift and walked carefully to the waiting taxi.

Back in the hotel room, she went straight to bed. She just took off her skirt, not bothering to get properly undressed.

'Ring them up and tell them we won't be home till Monday,' she said, raising her face about two inches from the pillow. 'We're having such a good time. Can you manage something like that?'

'Of course. Go to sleep.'

'Take the cover off. It's heavy.'

'Is that better?'

'Much.'

'Shall I get you some water?'

'Please.'

'Anything else?'

'They gave me some tablets. In my bag.'

I found the small envelope and handed her two according to the instructions. I brought her water. My hands were shaking.

'Shall I get you some tea?'

'Nothing else, thank you.'

'Right. I'll go to phone.'

'Poor Tess.'

The phone call home was easy. My father seemed delighted that we were happy together, my mother only anxious about whether my money would last out. 'Is Barbara there with you?' she asked me, probably longing to speak to her; she hadn't been home since Easter. 'Is she heck,' I said, too tired to elaborate, and my mother giggled, probably imagining me waiting for her outside shoe shops. And then the pips went.

When I got back, Barbara was fast asleep. Luckily I'd anticipated an evening in the bedroom and I'd bought two second-hand books, a pound of apples, a bar of chocolate and a carton of milk, so I was fairly comfortable. I crept to see Barbara from time to time. She seemed to be breathing normally but was still very yellow.

It was about eleven-thirty when she woke. I'd gone to the bathroom to wash, so as not to disturb her by running the taps, but unfortunately the plumbing in the next room made a noise like rushing rivers in the wall right behind her bed, which woke her.

I'd put out the light, but when I realized she was awake, asked her how she was. I asked her whether I could get anything for her, and to my horror she said she'd like a cup of tea, so I had to get dressed again and face going downstairs to the bar. 'Where can I ask for a cup of tea?' I remember saying to the barman, feeling that no one had ever before made such an outrageous request in an English hotel. 'Just ask here,' he said kindly, indicating the third button on his jacket, and in about five minutes had brought me a pot of tea for two and four plain biscuits. He said it was three shillings, and though I thought it a dreadful price, gave him five: I remember all my acts of generosity.

When I got back she was crying, I could hear her even outside the door. And I was absolutely shattered. I couldn't imagine such a thing. I don't think I'd ever seen her cry before.

'Oh please, Barbara, stop it, oh please.' I kept saying, 'Please don't cry. Look, I've got you a cup of tea, have a nice cup of tea. It's all over now. It's over. It's behind you. We'll never, never think of it again. We'll go home on Monday and everything will be all right. Mum and Dad are longing to see you, and you can show us all your new clothes and your shoes and everything. Oh please, Barbara. It's all over now.'

At last she stopped sobbing and lay back exhausted on her pillow. I mopped her face and her neck with my hand-towel and repeated my offer of tea.

'The abortion was nothing,' she said, angry at being so misunderstood. 'It was an episode. I didn't mind it a bit. I'm crying for *him*.' She started again.

That was too much for me. I poured out a cup of tea and drank it. I had a second. I ate all the biscuits. Then I got undressed again. I guessed there was more to come and there was.

'I love him. I love him. I thought he loved me.'

'Perhaps he does.' I cast round hopelessly for some straws

72

of comfort. He'd arranged the abortion and the hotel and everything, but that probably wasn't love but self-interest. I couldn't bring myself to mention even the pound theatre tickets though it was a lot of money. 'Perhaps he does,' was all I said.

'When I left, he said, "Perhaps you'll visit us again next summer." '

Even to my inexperienced ears that didn't sound like love. 'He didn't even ask me to write.'

'Oh Jesus Christ,' I said. It was the first time I'd ever used that particular name in vain, and was surprised how much it relieved my feelings.

'Pull your bed nearer mine,' Barbara said. 'I'm glad you're here.'

She cried almost all night. I kept drifting in and out of sleep, dreaming that I was in a small boat at sea, waking to find myself in a somewhat similar situation.

She stayed in bed next morning (I got her another tray of tea) but seemed more or less back to normal by mid-day. At least she looked marvellous again, and ate a good lunch. We went to the cinema in the afternoon and to another in the evening, and the following morning returned home. My father worried that she'd lost weight and my mother enthused about her French clothes and chic, but neither of them noticed the new wavering look in her eyes which I was aware of all the time.

Neither of us referred to the abortion or to 'him' ever again. But of course that weekend changed our relationship. Outwardly we're still distant, but we're both aware that she wanted me with her at that time.

Within six months she was engaged to a don: David Weatherby, a scientist. She married him in the same September that I married John. She seems happy.

I felt like ringing her up to ask whether she'd got over the Frenchman she'd cried over so bitterly all those years ago, nine years ago, but what was the point? I knew the answer. Like I knew that I'd never get over Victor. You can only cover things up, pile other things on top.

73

I heard Toby crying and went to him. He was very hot, his hair clinging damply to his little fat neck. Even as I picked him out of the cot he went on wailing. I took off his sticky pyjamas and took him into Dora's room where there was a spare bed, ready made up, and tucked him in there, between cool sheets, and recited nursery rhymes to him until he was comforted.

'Ba ba bang hee, Haby, haby wool,' he was singing as I left him.

John woke as I crept into our bedroom. He struggled to sit up. 'Was there a phone call?'

'No, there was not.'

'There never is,' he said, settling to sleep, and I felt full of pity for him again, and after getting undressed lay close to him and put my arm round him. I didn't know what to do. God, I didn't know what to do.

Chapter 9

The residents' association of Chestnut Close had arranged a barbecue for the first Saturday in September. We'd all paid ten shillings towards it. Walt and another man called Bernard Morrison were building the right sort of fire on the spare ground by No. 16, and someone else had managed to get an old-fashioned wind-up gramophone and a quantity of incredibly cheap red wine. Carole and I were baking bread rolls, Judy and Frances were making spiced sauces, and Pam and Elizabeth were making a special trip to a supermarket in Lewisham where they sold off all the meat cheaply at four o'clock every Saturday.

I was looking forward to the evening. I hadn't been out of the house since the holiday; Dora had also developed chicken pox and, unlike Toby, had had it very badly, even having spots in her mouth and at the back of her throat; I'd spent my days and nights entertaining and soothing her. John couldn't be persuaded to come, saying it was the sort of occasion he particularly disliked and that Dora wasn't well enough, in any case, to be left with a baby-sitter.

So, after putting the children to bed, I got ready, admitting to myself rather reluctantly that I wasn't too unhappy to be going alone. I planned to drink a great deal of the incredibly cheap wine and dance with whatever husband could be spared.

What to wear worried me. Western clothes, tartan shirts, suède waistcoats and blue jeans seemed to be the right gear, and I had no such garments. Finally I wore a long black cotton skirt and a fancy white shirt of John's and his blue cummerbund for good measure, hoping that I looked Mexican.

'What do you think?' I asked John, who was reading in the sitting-room.

'Exactly right.' He smiled, but it seemed an effort.

'Will you come just for a little while later on?' I was trying to be kind.

'If I must.'

'Of course not. You don't have to. There's not a bit of need. Please don't bother.'

But I'm too superstitious to leave in anger. 'Anyway, you know where I am if Dora wants me,' I added, and smiled at him.

Carole was nowhere to be seen, I didn't know whom to join. All the girls looked so thin and boyish in their tight shirts and trousers. Throughout my teens I'd longed to be small and boyish and I felt the desire choking me again. When I'm happy I feel all right, but alone on a bad evening I just feel fat. Elizabeth's husband, Mark, whom I didn't know very well, brought me a tankard of wine and said the food wouldn't be ready for half an hour. 'I'm slimming anyway,' I told him sadly.

'Everybody's always slimming,' he said, 'it's so depressing. Elizabeth is slimming and so is her mother and her grand-mother.'

(Elizabeth weighs about seven stone.)

'My daughter is slimming,' I said. (I'd made that up, want-ing to prolong the conversation.)

'How old is she?'

'Four-and-a-half.'

'Is she overweight?'

'Good heavens, no. She's perfect. Don't you know her? Dora Jilks. She plays with your Alison.'

'Oh, Dora. Yes, she is perfect. She always makes me think of Audrey Hepburn. Those eyes. Now, you're more the Signoret type. What's her name, Simone Signoret. Does anyone tell you that?'

'No one.'

'I am surprised.'

'Alison,' I said (I preferred to go on like this indefinitely to being left alone), 'is more the Julie Andrews type.'

'Do you know, you're right. That's never struck me but you're dead right. She *is* the Julie Andrews type.'

Mark gave me a warm smile and a fond reappraisal. 'The

Venus de Milo would be slimming today,' he said. 'And all those . . . Floras . . . do you know who I mean?'

I thought I did. Briefly I visualized acres of plump, pink nakedness. But it seemed safer to stick to film-stars. 'Elizabeth is more the Leslie . . .'

At this point Carole stuck her elbow into my side. 'I want you,' she said.

'Excuse me, Mark, I'll see you later.'

Carole's cheeks were flushed. 'Guess who's coming?' she said. 'Walt's boss. Isn't it the limit, and I was so looking forward to tonight and now I won't be able to relax for a minute. He phoned just before tea; he doesn't think Walt's ever entitled to a weekend in peace; wanting to know whether he could look over something by tomorrow, and Walt had to tell him about the residents' barbecue and how he was in charge of the grill and he said, "You know, that's the sort of thing I miss out on, that sort of neighbourly joie de vivre", and of course Walt said, "Well, why don't you drive over? We've got a lot of incredibly cheap wine and there's masses of food and someone's got some Caruso records", and he said, "Are you sure no one would object?" and Walt said, "Christ, no. Of course no one would object", and, oh God, here he is, and I'm depending on you, Tessa, because . . . Hallo, Victor, I'm so glad you could come. You remember Tess, don't you? Victor Fielding. Tessa Jilks. Look, I'll fetch you some wine. Don't go away. Walt's over there burning the food. Oh, look, he's seen you.'

Carole darted away. Victor waved at Walt, and Walt waved his fork at him and took off his chef's hat and waved that and did a little dance, and then Victor and I sat down together against one of the trees.

'I was afraid you wouldn't be here,' he said. 'Don't go away, please.'

After that we didn't speak to or even look at each other for a long time because Carole came back with some wine and Walt managed to leave his post and they talked about neighbourly joie de vivre and the community spirit and this is how it must have been in Olde England and how it was travel on

77

the Continent that was opening our eyes to the romance of eating outside and really the weather in England wasn't as bad as everyone liked to make out, people would make any old excuse if they were simply too entrenched in the idea of meat and two veg. to make the effort. Walt wanted Victor to meet Bernard Morrison who was the driving force behind the residents' association, my God, he was simply bursting with ideas, nothing was too much trouble for old Bernard, that was the marvellous thing, for instance he was even grilling the lamb with rosemary and Carole said Rosemary who and hoped Judy wouldn't get to hear of it and asked how Elspeth had enjoyed Greece and thanked them for their card, and then Walt was terribly sorry but he simply had to return to the line of fire and Carole asked whether we'd excuse her, only for as long as it took to toss the salad and hand out rolls and butter. And at last they left us.

'I was afraid you wouldn't be here,' Victor said. 'Don't go away.'

I can still remember the sounds and smells of the evening, the lights in the trees, people calling, laughing, talking with exaggerated animation and vivacity. I can still remember our silence in the middle of it. Amongst all the people, we sat in an island of silence.

'Do you like opera?' Victor asked at last.

'Not very much. Why?'

'I'm relieved. I'm prepared for anything, but opera would come hard.'

'What are we talking about? Why should you be prepared for opera?'

'I want to continue our relationship in a different way, that's all I mean. You broke off our previous relationship, presumably because you thought it was too physical, so we must change it. I'll work at anything. I've always worked for what I've wanted and now I'm going to work for you. What do you like to do? What are your interests?'

I couldn't decide how serious he was.

'What shall we do together? I know you're very intellectual, Tessa, Carole's always going on about it. I'm frightfully ignorant but I'm willing to learn. What do you like best? Ballet? Old Russian films? Do you like films?'

'Some films.'

'Good. The only film I've seen in the last ten years is *Citizen Kane*, which I thought was rubbish, but if you like films, we'll go to films, we'll become members of the National Film Theatre and go every Friday night. Unless you'd prefer the theatre.'

'Yes, I think I'd prefer the theatre.'

It was strange to sit with him, talking, not touching, the darkness coming down around us. I was honestly bemused. I had no clear idea, no idea at all, what the future held for us, if anything, but it didn't seem to matter while I sat there next to him.

'Poetry,' I said, for something to say. 'Do you like poetry?'

'To me poetry is an unplumbed sea. Is that a good line?'

'Promising. Shall I say some?'

'Please.'

' "The hour became her husband and my bride." '

They'd begun to serve the food. Everyone was called to the fire. There was an increase in the volume of chatter and laughter.

We were the only ones who didn't move.

'I think I'm going to find poetry tough going,' he said, 'but I'll crack it.'

I had two bread rolls and a large helping of green salad as well as a bowlful of cream cheese and walnuts which Judy Morrison had kindly provided for me, and Victor had a very small chop; like John, he obviously had reservations about barbecues.

'How could you put up with me so long,' he asked, 'when I didn't try to woo you?'

'You can't believe such rubbish.'

'I believe in facts. The facts are that you discontinued our

Friday meetings and reversed your decision about coming to see me at work. Facts.'

Carole was bringing round lemon meringue pie and a fresh lot of cardboard plates and plastic forks.

'It's fantastic,' Victor told her, 'I'm having a great time.'

She beamed and went off to tell Walter.

'Will you come to the theatre with me on Friday night, Tessa? From now on it shall be your way.'

I wanted to tell him that I preferred it his way, but then we would be back where we started and I was hazily aware that that wasn't where I was supposed to be.

I couldn't think and didn't want to. The warm night, his voice and nearness, my desire; it was a sort of union. I felt outside myself, in a strange element. If only it could go on for ever, I thought. It seemed like a state of grace.

(When I was eighteen I could put myself into a trance. It started accidentally. One morning I'd been working hard for my A-levels, learning a lot of boring facts for History until I could cram in no more. At about eleven I went downstairs for a cup of tea and my mother asked me to take out some washing for her – 'Just the thing to clear your brain,' she probably said – while I was waiting for the kettle. It was a windy morning, the sky bright blue and the clouds dazzling, the sort of whiter-than-white my mother's washing should have been but wasn't. I hung up shirts and towels and pillow-slips and then stood back and looked at the swaying apple tree and the clouds, and that did it. I wasn't thinking of God or infinity or Wordsworth's Prelude, but somehow of nothing. I'd put myself into an exalted state: it was like being an angel. It's difficult to describe a state of trance without assuming a mystical vocabulary, but at the time, having read little of such experiences, that was the phrase which came to me when I tried to describe it to myself afterwards – I have never tried to describe it to anyone else until now. I'm not sure how long the state lasted, probably only two or three minutes, during which I remained in the garden staring at the tree. Afterwards I had a lovely hour or so when the trance was over but the memory of beating wings was still strong. I now realize that that time is very like the post-orgasm stage, but then I was a virgin and had nothing but literature with which to compare it. It was beautiful enough for me to try it again the next morning, and it happened again. And the following morning. After that I got worried that I might be drawing on some expendable power, so I cut it to once a week. It never failed. All that summer I could get myself into a trance and enjoy the hour of heightened awareness which followed. I learned to make the most of these times. I listened to music, Elgar it was that summer, and it was the music of the spheres; I sniffed perfume, and it was the smell of paradise; I read T. S. Eliot and understood it.

When I went to University I forgot about my talent. That seems more incredible than anything else, but is also the simple truth.

Next summer I could do nothing. My temporary alliance with the force-that-through-the-green-fuse-drives-the-flower was over. I tried and tried when I was pregnant and doing psychosomatic exercises, but nothing, and yet again nothing. Nothing until the night of the barbecue, when I seemed near it again.)

Of course, it couldn't last.

'Will you, Tessa?'

'Will I what?'

'Will you come to the theatre with me on Friday evening?'

'I don't know, I really don't. I must have time to think. Not next Friday, anyway.'

'When?'

He had broken the spell, had managed to bring me back to a world of husbands and wives and children and impossible decisions.

I stood up. 'I'll let you know,' I said, unable to hide my disappointment.

And yet I loved him. I felt my blood racing, my stomach churning, my heart pounding as I stood looking down at him.

He stood up, then. He put his hand out to touch me but let

it fall. I could just see him – it was dark, the moon hadn't risen – his navy-blue suit and grey striped shirt (he'd made even less concession than I to barbecue attire) – tall, on the heavy side, dark, not particularly handsome, not as handsome as John. Why, then? Why this response to him in my blood and my guts?

How could it be different? That's how he happened to look, that's all, the man who'd spoken to me, roused me, made me. He could have been fat and sweaty; if so, that's what I'd have wanted.

'I'll let you know,' was all I said, though it wasn't what I wanted to say. I loved him miserably and utterly.

They'd had enough of Caruso and the wind-up gramophone and put a Beatles track on someone's portable tape-recorder. *Yesterday. All my troubles seemed so far away.* It seemed the saddest song in the world and the most beautiful. *But I believe in Yesterday.*

'Let's get some more wine,' I said.

'It's undrinkable.'

'I can drink it. Well, let's dance, then. Please.'

But now Victor was miserable; I'd made him miserable; as he stood close to me I could see the hurt look in his eyes. I suppose I might have relented then, but at that moment Elizabeth's husband appeared at my side, 'Come on, Judy, you promised me a dance,' and though I tried to get away from him, protesting tiredness and mistaken identity, he wouldn't let go of me and I gave up trying to get away as I saw Carole and Walt bearing down on Victor again.

'You've been long enough with that guy,' Mark said, 'Walt told me you'd spent all your evening looking after him and I reckon enough's enough. Don't you think you deserve a little fun now?'

Mark has small, protruding teeth and a cheeky smile which I could see even in the dark. For a time I tried to think of an insult offensive enough to penetrate his large insensitivity, but it defeated me and I had to be satisfied with standing on his feet whenever I could.

'Don't you?' he asked again, suddenly gathering me to him and pinioning me against the largest chestnut tree. I realized that I might have led him on a bit with the film-star game earlier on, so I didn't like to be brutal; I just pushed against him, which unfortunately excited him even more so that we stood there wrestling for about half a minute before he as suddenly released me, breathing very fast.

I decided to treat it as fun. 'I'll have to warn Simone Signoret about you,' I said, and he laughed and panted and took out a handkerchief to wipe his face. Oh, I could have slipped away then, but I didn't. We danced the next dance together in a friendly and formal way, and at the end he kissed me and said he'd better go to look for Elizabeth.

Victor seemed to have disappeared, I thought perhaps he'd gone home or to Carole and Walt's house. I sat on a log near the embers of the fire and was joined by Ruth O'Brian, a very beautiful girl, very beautifully and largely pregnant, who sat on the grass leaning back against me. 'Who was the man you were with?' she asked, with no preliminaries.

'Victor Fielding,' I said. 'He's . . .'

I was on the point of telling her that he was Walt's boss and that I was entertaining him on Carole's behalf, but decided not to.

'He's my lover,' I said, hoping she wouldn't believe me, that she'd think I was kidding.

'I thought he was.'

'Why?'

I felt her shrugging her shoulders. 'Don't you think one is extra sensitive when one's pregnant? I mean, tastes and smells and things are much more pronounced; I think intuitions are, too. When I saw the two of you tonight I said to myself, Ah, so that's why Tessa's been looking like the cat who's had the cream all summer. But now, poor Tess, it's over. Isn't it?'

'When's the baby due?' I asked, abruptly changing the subject.

'Not for another couple of months. Isn't it dreadful?'

'You look marvellous.'

83

'Christopher doesn't think so.'

'I bet he does.'

'Would you think he needed to have looked in on Charlotte seven times this evening?'

Charlotte was their daughter, aged two. Not being pregnant, I had difficulty not only about venturing an answer but even in understanding the question. Who could be baby-sitting? It was usually Ruth's mum. I gave it up.

'Isn't everything badly arranged? Don't you feel that?'

Whether she was referring to the barbecue, the baby-sitting, the reproductive process or to life in general, I wasn't sure. 'Shall I rub your back?' I asked.

She started to cry then, sobbing against my legs and drying her eyes on my skirt, and I went on rubbing her back and saying, 'There, there,' until she stopped, after which we sat in companionable silence.

People were starting to drift away. I could hear them collecting their various possessions; the records were being sorted out and the glasses and cutlery. I'd promised to help with the washing-up in Judy's, but hadn't done so.

Christopher came and heaved Ruth to her feet. 'What have you been up to, you and Tessa? You look very guilty.'

'Good night, love,' Ruth said, sounding fairly cheerful again.

'Time to go home, Tess.' It was Carole. She was standing in front of me with Walt and Victor. I got to my feet and we walked away, Walt and Victor in front, Carole and I behind.

'You must come in for a night-cap,' I heard Walt say.

'Thank you.' I hadn't heard Victor's voice like that before, completely dispirited.

May I come, too? I wanted to ask, but somehow couldn't bring myself to. I looked beseechingly at Carole but it was too dark for it to register. We came to our gate first so I had no option but to turn in and leave them. 'Good night,' I said.

Carole squeezed my arm, Walt told me to tell John that the committee would be refunding his ten shillings since he'd stayed away in the line of duty, and Victor said, 'Good night, Tessa,' without shaking my hand or pecking my cheek or touching me at all.

'Good night,' I said again, hoping it sounded tragic. I felt heart-broken. I wanted to call him back, but of course I didn't, just stood there aching for him.

It was a quarter past one when I went in. John had gone to bed but I was too strung-up to follow. I sat in the dark for a while, too miserable even to cry. Then I walked about the sitting-room telling myself that physical love didn't last, affection lasted and companionship, but not physical love. That was why I was so lucky not to have succumbed to it – well, I had succumbed – but to have broken away from it before it had overwhelmed my marriage.

John and I were compatible, liking the same authors, poets, politicians, newspapers (daily and Sunday), television programmes, films, breakfast cereals, instant coffee, holiday resorts. Wasn't that important?

Even more important, we had children (two) and had even considered another (almost everyone on the estate had two, so John favoured three).

It was the family that counted. I couldn't, shouldn't do anything which might split up the family. Dora had friends on the estate and had settled in at nursery school; Mrs Wright had even promised to have Toby as soon as he was out of nappies. If John and I separated, I should have to work – and what could I do? – probably have an unmarried mother (that's what everyone was having that year) living in. And what if Victor tired of me, would I drift to another lover, someone like horrible Bill Clarke, getting more and more indiscriminate until the inevitable run-down to financial insecurity, disillusion, and solitary old age? I was too cowardly to face such consequences. How I wished I could deceive myself into believing that I was being selfless, considering only the children or John.

What did I know about John? As far as I knew, he might be relieved if I left him. 'I think we ought to talk about our marriage,' I'd said to him when we came back from holiday, and he'd said, 'I know we should, but please, let's give it a few weeks until we do.' What was on his mind?

85

I went upstairs at last. First I went to see Dora and Toby who were both sleeping soundly, then I had a long, cool bath hoping it would relax me a little.

The moment I went into our bedroom, I knew John wasn't there. I put the light on, only to confirm what I already knew. He wasn't, and hadn't been, in bed.

Chapter 10

The first thing I felt was anger because he'd left the children —
Dora still far from well — unattended. If he'd been called out
he could easily have come to see me first, he knew where I was.

Then I felt envious because he seemed so much more free
than I; something or someone had beckoned and he'd simply
disregarded his responsibility and gone. I would never have left
the children alone.

Where had he gone? Had he received his long-awaited
phone call? It seemed too much of a coincidence that it
should have come on the first evening he'd been in alone.
Or had being on his own given him the opportunity to make
a phone call? That didn't seem to make much sense either,
since he was alone long enough at work every day.

I went downstairs again. I unlocked the front door and
looked out, though without expecting to see him. The estate
looked eerie and desolate in the greenish light of the sodium
lamps. There was not a sign of life, not even a little silent cat
walking along the paths between the gardens. Because of some
trick of the light, the houses seemed smaller than they usually
did, they were almost like huts, huts of a prison or a hospital
or a mental home. I seemed to be looking on a landscape I
knew from dreams. I started to shiver. Good God, where was
John? Where could he be?

After a few minutes at the door I felt angry again and went
back upstairs. I went to bed, but of course couldn't sleep.
There was something dramatic and final about his leaving the
house at that time of night with no explanation. We hadn't
quarrelled. I thought back over the day and couldn't find the
least hint of trouble; it had been a most ordinary Saturday.
He'd got up late, read *The Times* over his breakfast in the
kitchen, helped Dora with a jig-saw puzzle, gone out to the
bank and the library (I'd given him a shopping list but a very
short one) and come back in time for a late lunch. I tried to

remember what we'd talked about over lunch. The only thing I could recall was shoes; Saxone hadn't got his size in the style he wanted but were getting some in. Surely no one with plans to leave home could discuss shoes over lunch. In the afternoon he'd taken Toby for a walk as far as the railway bridge, and on the way back they'd stopped to see a bonfire in the garden of a house which was being demolished to make room for flats. He told me how excited Toby had been when the men had thrown on to the fire some old floorboards which had made the flames leap into the air. (Toby was still making bonfire noises when I put him to bed.)

So where did that leave us? I simply couldn't account for his disappearance. What should I do? Phone someone? Who? Surely not the police? Was he in trouble? I thought of the burglary we'd had, the men who'd ransacked our bedroom, it seemed so close. I didn't actually imagine that John was engaged in any criminal activity, but what if he'd got involved in something vaguely underhand and was afraid of discovery? Was he frightened about something? I tossed and turned.

Finally I took a sleeping pill; for me, with a life-long horror of all tablets, even aspirin, an extreme and desperate measure. (The only one I'd ever taken previously was on the night before Toby was born. I'd started having weak contractions at bedtime, and not wanting to spend the entire night awake and timing the wretched things as I'd done before Dora, took one of the sleeping pills the doctor had given me when I'd complained of being kept awake by heartburn. As a result I slept deeply until morning, when I woke to find the pains coming very strongly and hideously at two-gasp intervals, the hastily-summoned midwife and the baby arriving very soon afterwards in a dead heat.) This time, too, I went out like a light and slept late. Toby, who must have failed to wake me earlier, had crept in with me and fallen asleep at my side, and Dora was reading in her room. John hadn't returned.

I was having my first cup of black coffee when Carole called to return some forks and plates, and I had such a headache and such a sense of nightmare that I found myself telling her about John, which is the last thing I should have done, because she was so furious that it agitated me even more.

I thought I'd managed to calm her down over two cups of strong coffee, but all she did was go home and return with old Walt who started to march about the sitting-room talking about old-fashioned duty (bounden) and the weaker sex. Luckily, they had to leave quite soon because they were spending the day with Walt's parents at Bishop's Stortford. Before going, though, Walt assured me that if John was not back when they returned, he'd be bringing Carole to stay with me overnight – he's always very free with her services – and I said, 'Oh, things aren't as bad as that,' at which she gave me a hurt look.

My mother always phones at mid-day on Sunday and I was determined that she, at least, would get nothing out of me. However, when she made her routine enquiry about John I broke my resolve and told her just what had happened. Not only did I tell her about his disappearance but my voice started to quiver and thicken, so that she couldn't have been unaware of how upset I was about it.

She took some time over her response.

'People sometimes need to get away,' was what she finally came up with.

'Without so much as a note behind the clock!'

'I'll tell you what, I'll come up to keep you company.'

That depressed me. That she should think his absence as serious as that. She hadn't even come up for Toby's birth, leaving it to my mother-in-law to look after Dora and run the house.

'On Friday. I'm afraid I can't manage to get away before Friday. You see, I'm on Samaritan duty tonight and tomorrow night, and on Thursday evening, my dear, I'm compèring the fashion show we're putting on for Muscular Dystrophy.'

'I expect he'll be back by Friday.'

'I hope so. Do let me know if he is. Goodbye, love.'

Since my father's retirement, my mother had taken to keeping an egg-timer by the phone and, when the sand had run out, terminated any conversation without explanation or apology.

But five minutes later the phone rang again and it was my father. 'Would you like me to come up this afternoon? Your mother, as usual, is busy, but I'm quite free and should be very pleased to come.'

I felt weak with relief at his suggestion, and at the same time ashamed that I so needed him.

'I would, rather. The thing is that one or two of my friends have got to hear about his going, and if I'm alone they'll probably feel obliged to offer to stay with me. Isn't it silly!'

'When do you expect him back?'

'Dad, I know nothing about it; nothing. Only that he left the house last night while I was out and that he hasn't returned or got in touch with me.'

'Were you stunned when you realized he'd gone, or just surprised?'

'What an odd question. Stunned, I think.'

'Is he ill or in trouble? You must have some ideas about his disappearance.'

'No, I haven't. Not really. I mean, I knew he was unhappy, but that's all. Do you think I should contact the police?'

'What about close friends? Contact them first. We'll talk about the police when I get there.'

I phoned John's mother in Coventry. I thought it most unlikely that he would be there, but not impossible. As she didn't mention it, I couldn't see the point of worrying her about his disappearance so I talked only about the children, the chicken-pox, how pleased Dora had been with the colouring-books she'd sent.

'How's John?' she asked, when I'd already started on the goodbyes.

'He's not in at the moment.'

'Is he any better since the holiday?'

'The burglary upset him a lot.'

'You've heard nothing about that?'

'Nothing. John got the insurance people to call, so I suppose we'll hear something from them some time.'

I couldn't think who else to ring. As far as I knew, John had no close friends, only several colleagues, most of whom he seemed to despise or dislike.

We had bread-and-butter for lunch. The children weren't eating, anyway, and for once I wasn't hungry.

'When is Daddy coming home?' Dora asked me at about four o'clock. She was up and watching television.

'I'm not sure, he may be late.'

'No, he won't be late. He said he'd mend my doll's bed. He promised.'

'When?'

'Last night. I woke up with a sore mouth. I wanted you but Daddy came and he read to me.'

'What did he read?'

'*The Princess and the Pea.*'

'No, I read that to you before going out.' I wondered if her illness had confused her.

'Daddy read it again. I like that book a lot. And when he was putting it away, he fell over Patsy's bed and broke it and I cried and he promised to mend it tomorrow and that's today.'

'Then I expect he will. But if he doesn't get back in time, Granpa will, because he's coming later on.'

'Granpa is your daddy, isn't he?'

'Yes.'

'Is he any good at dolls' beds?'

'Fairly good.'

'Let me know when he comes.'

She went back to Pinky and Perky, repulsive pigs with squeaky voices which she watched every Sunday with grim fascination.

Toby was out on the terrace where I found he'd cut off

every geranium head from all my pots. I didn't even have the energy to scold him. I put them on a flat dish in the centre of the table, and for the rest of the day he kept climbing up to look at them, saying, 'Oh, pretty boy, Toby,' in a very self-satisfied way.

At half past five, my father arrived. And my mother, to my surprise, was with him. I was happy to see them and ashamed that I hadn't been home since Christmas. I gave up expecting to hear from John.

At first we were very gay, we laughed over Toby's antics and, when she wasn't around, at Dora's attempts at adult conversation. Mother told improbable stories about my father, and he, all-too-probable ones about her : how, on being asked to choose numbers out of the drum for the Lifeboat Institution raffle, she had managed to pick his out of 4759 for first prize; how she'd cycled home from the supermarket only to find her own bike safe in the garage. (This seemed a poor sequel to the famous account of how she'd left Barbara, at six weeks, in her pram outside Woolworth's, remembering about her only when unpacking her shopping and finding all the tins of milk powder.)

I put the children to bed and we had supper. My father mended Patsy's bed while I washed up, and my mother talked to us in turn.

Later she watched *Play of the Month* (Shaw) on television and my father and I talked in the kitchen. I told him how unhappy John and I had been all summer. I told him about Victor.

My father, who'd remained all his life very much the clergyman's son, can't have relished hearing about my affair or how it had come about, but he listened gravely, offering neither criticism nor advice.

'Well, you poor girl,' he said when I'd finished. That's all. No amount of bitter recrimination could have made me realize how sad a mess I'd made of my life.

We sat on in silence then; he smoking his pipe, I looking at the Sunday supplements. When the play, *Mrs Warren's Pro-*

fession, it was, had finished, my mother joined us. She found us in low spirits but didn't ask the cause – she doesn't believe that much goes on in her absence – and launched into an attack of the production she'd just watched, comparing it most unfavourably with the one given by the Woodfield Amateurs in 1956. Rosamund Hartley; didn't I remember her, her husband was the Physics master in the Boys' Grammar School, their only son played the 'cello in the Youth Orchestra, now she really brought tears to the eyes, was what my mother would call an actress. Of course they'd left the district, surely I knew, and what a loss it was. Yes, very sad, her husband had been involved in taking women's underwear from the gardens in Park Crescent, which seemed such a foolish thing to have done. If only he'd come to her, she could have given him any amount left over from various jumble sales, women's underwear never sells because you can't try it on, can you, well old Nancy Smith does but she's over ninety and who's going to stop her. Of course he said he was only borrowing it, but naturally people talked, so you can understand . . .

'Have you had any further thoughts about John?' my father asked her. (I'd forgotten how he would sometimes stop her in mid-flow.)

'Only this,' my mother said. 'If he's alive and well, then he's behaving very thoughtlessly.'

'If he'd been involved in a car accident, I'd surely have heard by this time,' I said.

'What could make a normal, decent person behave in such an uncharacteristic way?' my father asked himself and us, getting no reply.

'I keep on expecting the phone to ring. I keep on thinking there'll be some news. Do you think I should ring the police?'

My father looked at me as though considering the question, but when he spoke it was of something else. 'I ran away from home when I was eighteen. In the summer holiday. I'd won a theological exhibition at Edinburgh University, something quite modest, restricted to the sons of clergymen, something like that. My father kept saying I wasn't committing myself

93

to the Church by taking it, I could choose to teach instead or indeed choose any job with some spiritual significance, but I felt it was a commitment.'

'So you ran away,' my mother said. 'How strange that you've never told me before.'

'Haven't I? Ancient history, my dear. Of no interest.'

'How long did you stay away?'

'A couple of months. Only I let them know where I was almost immediately; within a few days. I went to work on a farm in Norfolk, near Teddy Hutchinson's place. They came to see me on the second or third Saturday I was there, I had the afternoon off and we went to the sea, quite a pleasant day, and as I was seeing them off at the station, my father asked me whether I'd ever had thoughts of going to a horticultural college; I got my way as easily as that.'

'And so you should have; it was your life.'

'I've never felt proud of it, though, running away without a word to either of them. My mother must have been very anxious about me. It's one of the things I regret.'

'I think it was brave. Don't you, Tessa? Don't you feel proud of your old father?'

'We'd got house-guests coming the next day, it must have made things very awkward for my mother.'

'I shouldn't think so. I dare say the house-guests took her mind off you quite wonderfully. Your father's people were very upper class, Tessa, they used to have important guests like Archdeacons, whereas on my side we just had aunties; very non-U. You married beneath you, Francis, you silly boy. If you had taken the theological exhibition you might have married Elizabeth Strickland-Batsford and had house-guests yourself . . . what other sort of guests are there, stable-guests? garden-guests? . . . or does "house" signify infesting the house, as with house-flies? House-guests? Anyway, I don't think he should stay up much longer, Tessa, do you, he's not as young as he was and he's got to look after Dora and Tobias tomorrow morning while you take me to Town. Oh, didn't I tell you? I've got to get a smart new suit because I've been chosen as delegate to the annual general meeting again this year, a bit of a bore, really, but I don't like to refuse. Your poor old father must have the spare bed; I'll be quite comfortable on the couch.'

She makes great play of being a few years younger than he.

I insisted that they had the double bed whilst I slept in the spare bed in Dora's room.

'So if the naughty boy does come home tonight, he'll find his bed occupied like poor Peter Pan,' my mother said when I went in to say good night. She looked young and pretty without her heavy make-up and stylish blue-framed glasses. She squeezed my hand.

When I got downstairs, Carole was at the door; they'd just arrived home. She was horrified that there was still no news of John. She called Walt over as he was passing from the garage and they both came in.

By this time we were all embarrassed by the situation. What else was there to say? Old Walt sat on the sofa with his mug of Nescafé and I could feel him longing to go home.

He suddenly thought of something to say and swung round towards me. 'Well, Tessa, you were certainly a brick last night. He kept on saying how well you'd looked after him, didn't he, Carole. Yes, I really think Fielding's got a lot on his mind at this present moment in time. Millicent, the P.R.O.'s sec., has a theory that it's to do with the Japanese project that he and the P.A. are working on, and she could be right. Anyway, we got him to forget his worries for a while, eh, Tessa? Did Carole tell you what he suggested for next Friday? He wants to take the three of us to the theatre, followed by supper at the Savoy Grill. He even suggested picking us all up here beforehand. I've got to sound you out about what play you'd like to see, Tessa. What about it?'

Somehow, I couldn't summon Victor to my mind. I didn't say anything.

'Leave her alone, Walt, for God's sake. We'll go home, love. Keep in touch.'

Chapter 11

I'd meant to get up early to ring the police before anyone else was up, but I overslept and when I eventually got downstairs, found my father boiling eggs, my mother making toast and Dora laying the table. It was already nine o'clock. Toby, who'd been playing farms since six and was now having his first nap of the day, was the only one still in bed.

When Dora was fetching the milk from the front doorstep I told my parents that I intended to ring the police after breakfast. 'Yes, I think you must,' my father said.

Dora came back without the milk. 'There's policemen on the path,' she said, and flew upstairs. For a moment I was afraid she was upset, but she was only making sure that Toby shouldn't miss them, he liked policemen even more than cows. As I went to the door I could hear him thumping downstairs, 'Where? Where?'

I was certain that they'd come to tell me that John had been involved in an accident, and couldn't understand why they were asking to speak to him.

'Well, he's not here,' I said. 'Where is he?'

'That's our question,' the older policeman said. 'Could you tell us where we can contact him?'

I explained to them about his being missing and how I'd intended ringing the police station immediately after breakfast.

'Won't you come in?' I said, conscious of Dora opening the door a fraction for Toby to peep out.

We were having breakfast in the dining-alcove (we usually had it in the kitchen but Dora was treating my parents to the best), so we had no privacy in the sitting-room and, to make matters worse, Toby came to join us. He was in pyjamas, his blanket trailing behind him, his thumb at the ready.

'Do you know a colleague of your husband called Adam Beauchamp?'

'I seem to know the name. I may have met him, I don't think so.'

'He was found dead in his flat late on Saturday evening and we have reason to believe that he committed suicide.'

'How frightful. Adam Beauchamp. How awful. What's it got to do with my husband, though?'

'We wanted to tell your husband that we recovered from his flat certain items which he reported missing from your house on the night of August 20th.'

'In Adam Beauchamp's flat?'

'That's right.'

'The silver frame and the transistor?'

'That's right.'

'How strange. Adam Beauchamp. I wish I could think who he was. I certainly know the name.'

'Along with a letter addressed to your husband. That's how we were able to trace the things to you so soon, though without the letter we would certainly have been able to do so in due course.'

'Yes.'

'Naturally we have to keep the letter until the coroner sees it. Your husband will be able to claim it afterwards.'

'So have you come simply to tell us that our things have been recovered?'

'We also wanted to ask your husband what he knew of Mr Beauchamp's activities. Obviously, after coming across in his flat certain items reported stolen, some routine enquiries have to be made. Have you any idea when your husband will be home?'

'I haven't. No. As I told you, I was about to ring the police. To ask them to check on hospitals in case he'd had an accident.'

'Since when has he been missing from home, Mrs Jilks?'

'Since Saturday night.'

'What time did he go out on Saturday night?'

'I'm not sure. You see, I was out at a party and he was in, baby-sitting.'

'And he wasn't in baby-sitting when you returned?'

97

'No.'

'What time did you return, Mrs Jilks?'

'About one o'clock.'

'One a.m. on Sunday morning.'

'That's right. And he'd gone.'

'Did he go by car?'

'Yes. I checked in the garage, yesterday.'

'Was it his car or yours?'

'His, I suppose; it was in his name. I always thought of it as ours.'

'Could you give us details of the car, please?'

'It's a green Mini Estate.'

'The number?'

'AUY 2 something something B.'

'AUY 287 B,' Dora said from the dining-room.

The younger policeman wrote it down. After that they stood looking at each other for a moment or two, and then both looked at me. 'Leave it with us,' one of them said. 'Got fed up with baby-sitting, probably,' said the other.

I saw them out.

'You needn't tell us what went on,' my father said, like Claudius to poor Ophelia, 'we heard it all.'

'We didn't understand any of it, though,' my mother said. 'But anyway, come and have your breakfast. This is very good marmalade, isn't it, Francis? Did I make it? I thought so.'

I drank my coffee and ate my toast and thought about Adam Beauchamp. My father was reading the paper, glancing at me from time to time. My mother was playing I-Spy with Dora and feeding Toby but giving me all her attention. I would have liked to explain something to them, but there was nothing of it I understood.

'Who is Adam Beauchamp?' my father asked, at last.

'I really don't know. I fancy I've met him but I can't think what he looks like. I've certainly heard John talk of him. He may have been a freelance script writer; someone John's worked with, something like that.'

I fetched our address book. His name didn't appear. I looked him up in the directory. His name, A. S. Beauchamp, was underlined. His address, 77c Henrietta Mews, S.W.6, told me nothing.

'I feel desperately worried now,' I told my parents after Dora had gone upstairs to fetch Toby's clothes. 'I just don't know what to do.'

'You could ring John's boss and ask him about Adam Beauchamp. He may be able to explain something,' my mother said.

'I wouldn't. That might implicate John in whatever made him commit suicide.'

We were all silent for a few moments, even Toby. (My mother had left the bowl of brown sugar within his reach and he was dipping fingers of toast, as well as other fingers, into it, and making discoveries: for instance, that the sugar stuck better on to the buttered side.)

'Could John be a homosexual?' my mother asked.

(And if he licked the toast before dipping it in, even more sugar stuck on.)

'That's an impossible question for Tessa to answer,' my father said, 'and I'm not at all sure you should have asked it.' (But if he licked the toast before dipping it in, they took the bowl away.)

'I don't know,' I said. 'I suppose it's possible. I've never really thought about it.'

(Dora came downstairs with Toby's clothes and stopped him roaring by hitting him sharply on the head.)

'It's struck me once or twice,' my mother went on, 'that he might be. But of course I didn't tell your father. I've got nothing against it, as you know, but it's certainly not what one would wish in a son-in-law. Well, I'll take Dora to the shops. I'll just have to make do with Bromley; I can see you're not going to take me to Oxford Street today.'

'Of course she's not. I'll take you and Dora to Bromley.'

'I don't want to go,' Dora said firmly. 'I want to stay with Mummy because she's worried.'

'I'm not a bit worried. Not a single bit. But I don't think you're well enough to go out yet. You'd better stay home with me.'

'I'm not offering to take Toby, dear. Last time he kept opening the changing cubicles and making everyone scream.'

My father and mother went out and I washed dishes with Dora and swept the kitchen floor and Hoovered the sitting-room and played with Toby and put him to bed and cleaned vegetables and worried about John.

At one point I went to his desk and started to look through his letters, but after the first, from a sixth-former in Manchester who'd enjoyed a programme about Coleridge, I felt too miserable to continue. I didn't want to find out that way.

Was John homosexual? The more I thought about it, the more probable it seemed. But if he and Adam Beauchamp had a homosexual relationship, why should Adam Beauchamp have burgled our house? If he had taken the silver frame, etc., in order to appear an ordinary burglar, what was it that he was really after? Evidence of something? Photographs? Something which John wouldn't return to him? But John didn't strike me as the sort of person who would refuse to return anything if requested to do so. I realized that I was thinking of John with considerable affection.

When *Play School* started at eleven, I settled down with a pencil to do some constructive thinking.

I imagined Adam Beauchamp arriving at our house, parking his car, or perhaps he'd come by the last train, breaking in through the french windows in the dining-alcove (the police had discovered quickly enough how the burglar had entered, there was a small broken pane of glass in the window through which he'd been able to unlock the door). I couldn't imagine how an amateur, and I presumed he was an amateur, could have had the nerve. Even if he knew, and I suppose he did, that we were away, he could so easily have been over-looked or overheard, the houses on the estate being so close together. It was only our bedroom which had been ransacked — I wrote 'bedroom' on my piece of paper and underlined it —

though the silver frame had come from the sideboard in the dining-room. Why was he so sure that whatever he was looking for was in the bedroom rather than in the desk in the sitting-room where John kept his papers? The policemen, the ones who'd come after the burglary, had been surprised that nothing had been taken from the sitting-room, they thought some of the small prints and one or two of the ornaments would have been very easy to pick up and dispose of. I thought it possible that Beauchamp had gone upstairs without even going into the sitting-room; I underlined the word 'bedroom' again; but what did he want?

I was suddenly desperately afraid that John might be on the point of committing suicide himself, or had already done so. Oh, John, please don't, I wanted to tell him, please don't. Nothing matters. Whatever you've done, we'll get over it, we'll face it together. What a faithful little wife I seemed to be now that it was too late.

The phone rang. It was John's immediate superior, Hugh Trent, wanting to know what was the matter with him and when he'd be back at work.

'I don't know,' I told him. 'The thing is, I haven't seen him since Saturday night. He just went out. On Saturday night. I haven't seen him or heard from him since.'

Hugh was so completely thrown that he didn't ask another question, but spent the next minute or two telling me how I was not to worry and how he was quite sure that John would very soon be back and that there was a perfectly simple explanation if we could only think of it. 'I'll get Marilyn to ring you,' he said. (His poor wife, Marilyn, always seemed to be undergoing some new and uncomfortable form of psychiatric treatment, though there was nothing much wrong with her as far as I could tell, except a reluctance to mix with people, and being married to Hugh. She had talked to me once or twice and had even visited me briefly when Toby was born, so that Hugh always made out that I was her one and only friend. He liked everyone to realize how very great and gracious he was to stick by his neurotic wife, and couldn't leave her – and her most recent therapy, as a rule – out of any conversation, however brief.) 'Thank you,' I said, 'I'd appreciate that.'

When *Play School* finished I phoned Carole and asked her over for coffee. I was pretty sure she'd have seen the policemen, so I felt I ought to give her an edited version of what had happened.

We're quick to imagine that others are as interested in our problems as we are ourselves. When Carole came she didn't ask about John or the policemen. She'd had a phone call to say that the baby she and Walt had been trying to adopt for over two years was ready for collection at three o'clock.

I said that we must have a drink to celebrate, but she refused to consider it. 'Oh, no, please, just coffee, black coffee. I've been studying Spock and my other books all morning and my head's in such a whirl. Thank goodness you've had your holiday; oh, Tessa, you'd have to cancel it otherwise. Can I practise a nappy on one of Dora's dolls? Oh, if you knew how frightened I am. Labour pains can't be worse than the ones I've had all morning, and I haven't even learned how to breathe, and Walt's had to go to bed with one of his headaches, and what if he isn't well enough to drive. He's only ten days old. God, I've got to go to the lavatory again. I'm sure they won't give him to me if I don't calm down and how can I calm down when I know I'm going to be a mother, and, Tessa, I've wanted to be a mother since I was eight. We're going to call him Luke. Yes, I know I've said Timothy all along, but this morning I thought Timothy was rather ordinary and what if people called him Tim. Don't you think Luke is more dignified; for when he's a man, I mean. Professor Timothy Meadows? Dr Luke Meadows? Yes, I definitely prefer Luke. Luke. Don't you?'

Dora brought down her largest doll and I got a clean nappy and two safety pins, but however many times I demonstrated she couldn't manage it, though Dora could and was maddening about it.

'Look here,' I said, 'I've got some disposables left over from the holiday and you don't need a pin with those.'

For a long time I searched, but failed to find the Paddi-pads

I knew I still had. At last it occurred to me that they might still be in one of the suitcases that we kept on the wardrobe in Dora's room. I got a chair. But they weren't in the large black or in either of the smaller green ones. I was so annoyed and agitated by this time that I found myself looking even in the old zipped hold-all which we hadn't, in fact, taken away; hadn't used for years. It was, of course, empty. Except for four small envelopes each containing ten to fifteen tablets which I recognized as purple hearts. Why ever should there be purple hearts in our house? Neither John nor I had ever taken drugs. I was almost overcome by fear; I was convinced that they were significant in some way. But how?

When Dora called saying she'd found the nappies in one of the kitchen cupboards, I could hardly bring myself to go downstairs, I so wanted to fathom it out.

'I hope you won't mind our cancelling the theatre date with Victor,' Carole said when I got back to the sitting-room.

For a minute I couldn't think who Victor was; that's the state I was in.

'I mean, you don't wait two years and two months for a baby and fill in all those forms and get confirmed and everything just to leave him with a baby-sitter, do you? I can't imagine that Walt and I will ever go to the theatre again.'

'Oh, I don't know,' I said. 'In six or seven years' time you'll be able to take Luke with you.'

She took me quite seriously.

'Of course, you'll have to stick to the Sooty Shows for a year or two.'

'Oh, yes.'

My parents came home just before one. My mother hadn't succeeded in getting the suit she wanted, but had done very well in the new delicatessen in the High Street, so I didn't have to cook after all. Dora was full of the new baby who was expected and Toby kept trotting off to look in his old pram in the cloakroom to see whether it had come.

My father had a copy of the *Standard*. He showed me a

three-line paragraph about Adam Beauchamp, that he'd been found dead at his flat. It described him as a writer.

'No news of John?' my mother asked.

'Nothing.'

'At least you were trained for work,' my mother said, 'not just for marriage, as I was.' She was casting me as a single parent already.

'Rosemary's mother says that in *Tender is the Night*,' I said. 'I'm just reading it.'

'I'm sorry for her, then.'

'Good Lord, you never stop working. Do you ever have any free time?' my father said.

'All those things I do because I haven't got the qualifications for a proper job, a worthwhile job. Why should I stay home scrubbing and darning?'

'Scrubbing and darning,' my father said mildly. 'Scrubbing and darning. Now when . . .'

'There's a Women's Movement in America,' my mother said, 'and I'd like to join it.'

'As long as you don't have to go to America,' my father said. 'But I expect you can start something in Bridgeton. After all, you've got several things going over the years, haven't you?'

'How about us all making a sort of garland,' I said after lunch. 'With "Luke" in big letters in the middle. We could put it on their door by the time they get back. Wouldn't it take our minds off things!'

My mother and Dora were thrilled with the idea. I had a roll of white lining paper left over from the sitting-room ceiling and we mixed poster paints; sky blue, orange and pink, and my father, who wasn't thrilled, but as usual co-operative, pencilled in the lettering, my mother painted it, and Dora cut out petals from tissue paper (lime green) which I made into flowers and pasted round the edges, while Toby pasted the pages of his books together and ate rather a lot of the tissue paper, probably mistaking it for lettuce; he can't have liked it, but neither does he like lettuce.

We worked for almost an hour. The letters didn't stand out enough so we had to outline them with black, and by that time we were getting tired so that the whole thing became rather smudged, and we had to make more flowers to stick on. But finally we felt we'd done as much as we could with it, and we all went out and fixed it on their door. It looked pretty awful. Anyway, it got us through the afternoon.

And when the children were in bed, I received the summons I expected to No. 9 and that was much better than puzzling and worrying and waiting for a phone call. I found Carole's state of panicky ineptitude rather endearing, Walt's newly assumed role of infant psychologist not.

'Piaget,' he said as I went in, raising his head and indicating his large book. 'Now he regards learning and development as an active process, the child taking into himself from his environment whatever he needs and can assimilate at any particular stage, so that the task of parent becomes one of trying to understand the process taking place in his mind and providing him with appropriate . . .'

'Someone described the consciousness of the new-born baby as a great blooming confusion,' I said, trying to keep my end up.

'William James,' Walt said. ' "One big blooming confusion"; of course William James is old hat by this time. Have you ever thought how . . .'

Carole signalled to me behind Walt's back. 'Excuse us a minute, Walter.'

She led me upstairs and into the room which they'd been decorating and redecorating for over two years. At present it had white walls, white broderie-anglaise curtains and lamp shades, pale grey vinyl tiles, forget-me-not blue rugs, several very large soft toys which no baby would be able to lift for at least two years, a cot swathed in white tulle, pale yellow chest and cupboard and bath and toilet basket.

She stood by the door looking stricken.

I half expected a frightful confession : the baby wasn't up to the nursery, he didn't look like they did in the adverts, she couldn't seem to take to him, but no, all she did was utter a small sound, something between a sigh and a gasp, and lead me to the cot.

And there he was, hardly raising the snow-white covers; a tiny head on the pillow, a tiny hand. 'He's beautiful,' I said. I couldn't really see him in the dimmed light but he was beautiful all right.

She touched my hand and whispered very softly, 'Timothy.'

'What?'

'Timothy. As soon as I saw him I knew he was more of a Timothy. What do you think?'

I got closer to him, so close that Carole got nervous and pulled me back.

I nodded my head vigorously and she took me out of the room.

'He's beautiful,' I told Walt.

'What's that?'

'He's beautiful.'

'Oh come, come, Tessa. You can't really pretend that a human baby, ten days old, has any pretensions to *beauty*. Come, come.'

He was as delighted as she was.

Walter was further explaining the concept of what Piaget called sensori-motor intelligence when the first wail sounded. One advantage of having a baby in hospital is that you get, in a week or ten days, fairly used to the crying, fairly inured. Carole, of course, was totally uninured. She sprang to her feet and said, 'I don't feel I can cope,' and burst into tears, and Walt started to mumble, 'But all the early satisfactions are . . . his interactions with the world are . . . er . . . All we have to do at the moment is to take the bottle from the bottle-warmer and . . .'

'Nappy!' Carole shrieked, her hand on her heart, her voice and manner like a tragedienne crying 'serpent'.

'Look, I'll do it,' I said, 'I'm used to it.' And we all went upstairs.

Chapter 12

Everything was changed. Something momentous had happened and I was desperately miserable about it. I wanted John back, that's all I knew. As soon as he'd gone, I wanted him and only him. I don't pretend to understand, I certainly can't hope for sympathy, I'm just reporting the facts. As soon as John walked out of my life, I wanted him back.

I'm not sure why. I suppose I was afraid of being left on my own, the odd one out, a woman whose husband had deserted her; afraid of what people would think and say, afraid of the stigma attached to it.

If it had happened this year, I don't think that part of it would have been of such importance. Women are beginning to question the old values, being a spinster or a deserted wife are not such tragedies now. But ten years ago girls like me hadn't begun to think; for centuries we'd been conditioned to fear being on the shelf, and my God we feared it. 'She'll never get a husband,' we'd say about some poor girl because her face was too round and amiable or her legs too thick, but we never, never thought that any man could possibly fail to get a wife, however feeble his mind, protruding his ears or smelly his feet.

I'd got myself a husband and without too much trouble, and I didn't want to lose him. He was presentable, even hand-some – I couldn't put out of my mind his beautiful pale green eyes and his cleft chin – and moreover intelligent, well-read, well-informed, and I'd got used to women who doted on fools. However much I thought about the disagreements we'd had, particularly during the last year, it still seemed to me that he rated higher as a husband than almost any other I knew. He was considerate. He helped with the children. When Toby was born, he had started putting Dora to bed, bathing her and reading to her. He washed nappies. He took blankets to the launderette. When it was needed, he did the shopping. He was scrupulously fair about money. Walt gave Carole housekeeping, which seemed to me utterly degrading, and my college friend, Jane, had a husband who drank heavily while their children wore plimsolls all winter. My sister Barbara's husband expected her to do the shopping and the cooking, though they both worked full-time, she in a slightly higher position than he. (John – without any prompting from me – had tackled him about it on our last visit to Oxford. 'Ah, she likes all that,' David had said blithely. 'Women need to fuss about the house and the meals; it's a biological fact, old chap. No, she wouldn't have me doing any of it.')

John was, on the whole, dependable. For the last months, admittedly, he had been in the grip of an obsession about some-one – and I felt more and more sure that it was Adam Beau-champ – but it was an untypical state and the fact of its being so clearly an obsession made it more excusable. He wasn't the sort to misbehave with anyone available. I didn't feel unsure of him on every social occasion like so many wives of their husbands.

Whoever I thought about, John seemed superior. I wanted to contact him, tell him I understood what had happened to him, see if it wasn't possible to start again. After all, we were good friends, we cared for each other. There was too much between us to give up without a struggle. Even without love, and I couldn't pretend a great love on either side, it was better than the loneliness and panic I was feeling since he'd walked out on me. I felt lost.

I was very sorry that I'd told my parents anything about John's absence; I was finding their presence difficult. They, particularly my mother, wanted me to act, to ring people, to get to the bottom of things, whereas I preferred the idea of waiting until I could get in touch with him directly, being at home if he rang or came back; I didn't want to hound him.

My father must have sensed how I felt because he persuaded my mother to go back for her fashion show, and though he stayed on, he left me alone.

The night my mother went back, it was Wednesday night, four days after John's disappearance, I contacted the

Samaritans. I can hardly believe now, ten years later, that I had sunk into such despair. Perhaps it was partly that my mother spoke so much and so enthusiastically of them. (She had only recently joined them and one of the things that impressed me was the quite uncharacteristic modesty and gravity with which she spoke of the part she'd so far played, only saying that she felt she had been some help to one middle-aged woman who usually rang her on a Friday night when her husband was out.) It was also, I suppose, a desire to milk the situation of its drama, 'the female of the species wallowing in calamity, while at the same time working it like a mine rich in precious ore'. Colette.

I remember that it took me some minutes to summon up enough courage to ring the number I'd found in the local directory. It was almost midnight; I'd waited for my father to go to bed.

A man's voice, a gentle country voice, answered.

'I'm in trouble,' I said. It sounded corny the way I said it; I don't think I'd ever used the words before and I couldn't help my voice trembling a bit.

'Tell me about it.' I suppose it was the stock response, but it seemed immensely comforting, the invitation to confide in the perfect stranger. He listened to the whole sad story without interruption. At one point I was afraid he'd fallen asleep; I pictured him in bed, the phone dropping out of his hand, his mouth falling open.

But at last he spoke. He told me that he thought I should tell the police about the tablets I'd found in the hold-all in Dora's wardrobe. 'Mightn't they have been what Beauchamp was after when he burgled your house?' he said.

'I thought of that, but if I told the police wouldn't that implicate my husband in his suicide?'

'Does your husband take drugs?'

'No, at least I'm pretty sure he doesn't.'

'So he might have persuaded his friend to give them up and might have taken charge of them to keep them out of his reach.'

'Wouldn't he have got rid of them, in that case?'

'Perhaps he'd promised not to; promised his friend that he'd return them if he was ever in desperate need.'

'And perhaps we were on holiday when he did need them.'

'So that his friend broke into your house.'

'It doesn't sound quite right. I think they're quite easy to get hold of, purple hearts; he'd surely have got another supply. It's not as though it was heroin or something.'

'Are you certain what they are?'

'Yes. I've been offered some at parties.'

'We simply don't have enough information. We simply don't know what can have happened. Perhaps your husband didn't know, either. Perhaps he imagined he was somehow the cause of his friend's suicide; that could be enough to account for his disappearance.'

'He might have committed suicide himself.'

'Don't think about that. The facts we have are depressing enough, try not to imagine anything worse. How are you coping with the house and the children?'

'Fairly well.'

'That's wonderful. Do they ask for your husband?'

'Not much. The little one forgets anyone who isn't actually present, and Dora, well, she thinks John's on holiday or something and that my parents have come to stay instead.'

'I'm glad your parents are with you. Grand-parents are a tremendous help to the children if there's trouble between parents.'

'Not such a help to the parents, though; they're too involved.'

'That's why I'm glad you rang me. Why exactly did you ring? Was the worst thing, the fear of your husband's death?'

'No, I don't really believe he's dead, though of course I can't stop thinking about the possibility. My real fear is that my marriage is over.'

'It doesn't sound to me as though it is. Men have love-affairs which overwhelm them for a while but eventually they often decide that their wife and children are more important.'

'Yes.'

'You don't think it's likely in your case?'

'I'd like to think so. I'd like to be able to let him know that I'd be ready to start again. You see, when he did intimate that he did care for someone else, I promptly went out and had an affair myself. I didn't do it purposely, I mean, it wasn't tit-for-tat, it just happened that way. It was the first time anyone had suggested it and since he – I mean my husband – seemed to want me to have a life of my own, it seemed too good an opportunity to let pass.'

'Yes, I see. How long did your affair go on?'

'Seven weeks. After that I realized my husband was very unhappy and broke it off.'

'Your husband was very unhappy about your affair?'

'No, about his. He didn't know about mine, though I told him afterwards.'

'What did he say when you told him?'

'He didn't seem to care too much. He said it was ironic, that's all he said. I don't think he cared much.'

I'd started to cry and I don't think my Samaritan could hear much of what I was saying, though he let me continue.

After a while he said, 'We don't understand anyone completely. Perhaps you didn't understand how your husband felt, perhaps you misread the signs, perhaps he knew more than he admitted, perhaps he was angry, perhaps he was jealous. We don't know. We don't know what made his friend commit suicide or what despair made him walk out on you. We don't know, and it doesn't do much good to wrestle with the facts we think we know, torturing them into all sorts of fantastic shapes. The best thing is to take tomorrow as it comes, don't look beyond getting through the day. Go to bed now and try to sleep, don't hang on to your worries, let them go. Ring me again. Evening is the best time for me, but if you feel desperate they'll put you through to me at any time, day or night. Perhaps you'd let me have your telephone number, then if I'm not immediately available when you ring, I'll be able to get in touch with you as soon as I can.'

I gave him my telephone number and thanked him for listening to me. (One's personal Samaritan is called one's

Befriender. I found it enormously cheering to have an official Befriender.)

I can't understand now why I was in quite such anguish about John. Somehow I was no longer aware of his shortcomings; I thought of him as the boy he'd been when we'd first met, not as the man he'd become. I kept remembering the beginning of our relationship, how comforting his friendship and protection was at a time when everything and everyone was strange. I felt very much as though I was still the undergraduate I was then, incapable of dealing with all the hectic processes of life on my own. I was in a house I had chosen on a small estate where I knew everyone, my father was sleeping in the spare bed in my son's room, yet when I opened the curtains to look out before going to bed, I felt totally estranged, as though I'd newly arrived in a Moscow or Washington suburb.

I can't understand, now, why I didn't try to draw some comfort from the knowledge that Victor, older and more capable and protective than John, still cared for me. I simply couldn't think about Victor. He seemed to have become inextricably bound up with all the sordid aspects of the last weeks; John's humiliating love for someone who didn't love him, the burglary, the suicide, John's disappearance. When I thought about him at all I realized that I was being unfair, but I couldn't help it. My love for Victor couldn't take the strain, I admit it.

One morning he phoned me. 'Tessa,' he said, 'is that you, Tessa?' and the only thing I felt was disappointment that it wasn't John, and put the telephone down without a word. It was yet another ending.

The next morning I got the electricity bill. It was very large. (The architects of our estate had experimented with a new form of electric heating which was fairly efficient but enormously expensive to run.) I can't remember the exact sum but I know it corresponded almost exactly to the one we had in our bank account.

'I'm broke as well as everything else,' I told my father, passing him the bill with his coffee.

'We can lend you a few bob.'

'I must get a job. What can I do? If only I'd done my teachers' training . . . But I suppose I could apply for a place and a grant for this year. There's a college at New Cross. They're pretty desperate for teachers. Do you think it'll be too late? What could I do with Dora and Toby? I know Mrs Wright would take Dora full-time and she's starting at the Primary School after Christmas, but what about Toby? I'll have to go to see her. And who'll look after them for the rest of the day? I probably wouldn't get back until about five every evening.'

'I could stay for a week or two.'

'I'll have to phone everyone this morning to try to get something fixed.'

'Would it help if I took Dora and Toby to the park?'

'Oh yes, please.'

Stirred to definite action, full of plans, I felt much better.

Dora came downstairs still dressed in vest and pants. 'You'll really have to . . .' my father said, and stopped himself. I knew what he meant. My mother had been incensed by the amount of time and attention I gave to dressing Dora every morning. 'I never let you and Barbara play me up like this,' she'd said, and it was true. We'd been wartime children. I can only remember Barbara's cast-offs which had been originally made from something else; the bodice and sleeves from a blouse of Aunt Lucy's and the skirt from one of cousin Mabel's dresses. 'There was no point in my being fussy,' I'd said. 'I had nothing to choose from. I only remember ever having two new dresses and they were both old.'

Dora had many, many dresses. She loved clothes and I loved buying them for her, probably a reaction to the austerity I remembered, and every morning there was a fairly lengthy collaboration between us as to what she was going to wear, what frilly blouse with what pleated skirt with what socks and what shoes or sandals; various things would finally be laid out together on the carpet in her room and often when I'd left her alone to get dressed, I'd find that the whole scheme had been abandoned and quite another adopted, but since nursery school didn't begin until half past nine, it seemed as good a way as any to fill in the time.

'There's a button off my blue dress,' she said.

'But hadn't you decided on the yellow one with daisies?'

'I did put it on.' She stopped and looked mournfully at me.

'Have you had your breakfast?' my father asked.

'Yes.'

'Yes, what?' I said.

'Yes. Weetabix.'

'Yes, thank you, Granpa.'

'I didn't know the Weetabix was Granpa's. Thank you, Granpa.'

'Pretty boy, Granpa,' Toby said, smiling like an angel and patting his hand.

'I put my yellow one on, but I looked like Emma Price in it. I would like my blue-and-white, please, if you could sew on the button.'

'Mummy's very busy this morning,' my father said.

Toby came round the table to see what I was doing.

'I could wear my white skirt but none of the blouses I like are ironed, that's the thing.'

'What about your sundress?' This one I'd vetoed on account of the cooler weather.

'Oh yes. Thank you, Mummy.' She rushed upstairs.

'I'll really have to do something about her,' I said, 'I know I will.'

'She'll grow out of it.'

'Vethy pretty boy,' Toby said when she came downstairs in her strapless green sundress.

I decided to ask Carole about having Dora and Toby. She'd given up her job, of course, because of the baby, so might welcome the few pounds I'd have to give her. I worked out that I'd be able to drop off Dora and possibly Toby at the Nursery School on my way to the station, and that she might be able to work in fetching them with Timothy's walk.

After washing the dishes, I went across to see her. I found her in tears.

Carole wasn't a girl much given to tears. Indeed, I'd always considered her remarkably stoical. She'd gone through a great deal in the years I'd known her. Intercourse with Walter on the dot of ten every Saturday morning, which some pundit had worked out as the most likely way of her conceiving; every other Saturday; once a month when her temperature was lowest or highest with her legs stuck up on a couple of cushions; once a month with her legs up on cushions, remaining in that position for several hours or was it several minutes? (luckily Walter didn't have to stay with her but was able to get on with the Saturday chores); intercourse, again of course with Walter, at the infertility clinic, not perhaps overlooked but certainly inspected a few minutes later; all this she had borne with remarkable fortitude, yet the tiny, good baby she had so much desired was proving altogether too much for her.

'Oh, Tessa, he's crying again,' she said as I went in. 'What can I do? Don't you think I ought to give him some gripe water?'

'That doesn't sound like pain crying,' I said. 'That's just his company voice; he's just letting you know he's there.'

'No, he's in pain,' she said, 'he's puckering up his little face. Come and see.' She pinched my arm hard in her distress.

I followed her upstairs. The nursery was assuming a different look; piles of towels and dirty nappies strewn all over the floor, even on the fluffy rugs, a clutter of empty coffee mugs and open books on the changing table, grey, solid-looking water in the bath, wads of used cotton-wool everywhere.

'He messes everything,' she said. 'Nobody told me about nappies. I mean, that you can't get it off. That it's bright yellow and sticks like mustard and you can't get it off.'

Her voice had taken on a high, hysterical note I hadn't heard before.

'All his lovely dresses and his shawls and everything. Now I understand why they try to sell you all those yellow baby clothes, and to think I insisted on having everything white.'

The devastation was certainly horrific. I looked away.

'You're probably giving him far too much,' I said.

We went to the crib. His face seemed old with crying, as though he'd been at it for years and years. Carole picked him up and put him over her shoulder.

'I pat his little back for hours after every feed,' she said. 'I don't know what else I can do.'

'You're thumping him,' I said.

'What do you mean? I'm just getting his wind up.'

'That's only for mothers who don't nurse them; you know, the babies who're just fed and shoved straight back in the cot. When you nurse them and carry them about and fondle them, they get their wind up in a natural way, you don't have to do all that.'

'This is precisely what I've been told to do.'

'Try it without.'

'I certainly won't. All my books say it's absolutely vital.'

'I'm only trying to help, Carole. You're in a bit of a state so you don't realize how hard you're hitting him; he's not Walter. There, now you've got another dirty nappy.'

We both looked at him. His face had become red and passionate, he looked like a very small and angry Bertrand Russell. We waited for him to finish.

'I'll change him,' I said. 'I'll show you how to do it.'

'I can do it perfectly well myself.' She swung him away from me.

'No, you can't. Look how it's oozing through.'

'Oh God, oh God. I spent ages fixing that one. Oh God. You take him, for God's sake. Oh God.'

So I took him and laid him on his posh changing pad among the coffee cups, and peeled off his outer garments and his plastic pants and his nappy and nappy liner and swabbed him down and washed him and patted him dry.

He was still crying, but quite gently now; his face was pink and mottled, his lips turned down at the corners. He was thin and rather ugly, his legs bent like a frog's, his small hands raked the air as though calling down curses on both of us.

'Send him back,' I said. 'You're not stuck with him yet.

You've got another month to change your mind.'

'I think I will,' she said, picking him up and holding him to her face as though he were a bouquet and kissing his little concave chest. 'I think I will.' He peed down her neck but she didn't seem to mind.

It was a long time before she'd give him back to me. When she did, I fixed his nappy in a different way but she thought he looked uncomfortable and undid it.

'I'd better go. I'll come again tomorrow.'

I didn't mention Dora and Toby. I knew she wouldn't have time for anything but changing nappies and thumping for at least six months.

Chapter 13

'Of course, you realize that all our places have been filled since last July. It's only because of your very special circumstances that I decided to see you.'

'It was very good of you.' I hoped I sounded sufficiently ingratiating.

'And your subject at University?'

'French with first-year English.'

She wrote something on a piece of paper, then checked the information with the form I'd filled in.

'French,' she said, and after a very long pause, 'with subsidiary English.

'And you got . . . er . . . ?'

'A third,' I said, since she seemed too embarrassed to get it out.

She looked down at her hairy grey cardigan as though seeing it for the first time. I found myself staring at it too. I'd gone in to the interview determined to appear bright and out-going – Walt had been round the previous evening and had treated me to a dissertation on interview techniques in which the words bright and out-going had figured largely – but after two or three minutes with Miss Hammond I felt old and sad. And I couldn't think of anything but her great, grey hand-knitted cardigan. How many stitches, I wondered, had gone to spanning that formidable girth? The buttons were grey mother-of-pearl which reminded me of my grandmother who had such a buckle on a black dress. 'What's that?' I used to ask her. 'Mother-of-pearl,' she used to say, slowly and deliberately, teaching me the word. (I wasn't quite three at the time; it was just after my grandfather died. When I reminded my mother of the dress afterwards she said it had come from Derry and Tom's and had cost eighteen-and-eleven and ten clothing coupons.)

'Quite so. French and first-year English.'

She gave me a much more cheerful look. 'Do you feel you could teach Junior School Mathematics?' she asked.

'Oh yes,' I said. I tried to elaborate but failed. I got grade 6 in O-level Maths, which didn't seem worth mentioning.

'Remedial teachers are in very short supply. Do you find you relate to backward children?'

'I like all children.' That seemed a safe answer.

'Do you interest yourself at all in educational psychology?'

'Oh, I do. Gosh, yes.'

'You have . . .' Her eyes wandered over my form again while mine wandered over her cardigan, front left and front right. (I'd once knitted a cardigan for Dora and that had taken months and months.)

'Two children,' she said at last.

I admitted it. 'Yes. A girl and a boy.'

'Two children. A girl and . . . er . . . a boy. Mrs Jilks, if I admit you to the East London and Kent Training College on 27th September, what arrangements do you have for the welfare of your girl and your . . . er . . . boy?'

'My son will be in the charge of a neighbour who has a daughter roughly the same age.'

'Your neighbour feels able to cope with the two young children roughly the same age?'

'She certainly does. Yes.'

'How . . . fortunate.' (Occasionally she seemed to pounce on a word, as though it were a mint, rolling it slowly round her mouth.)

'My daughter goes to Nursery School, she's starting at Primary School after Christmas, and she'll stay with another neighbour for the rest of the day.'

She suddenly leaned towards me. 'It's very modern, isn't it?' she said. 'Your career. Of course I'm rather ancient, I was at University soon after the end of the First World War, very old-fashioned. Do you think it's a better way? Having a taste of marriage before graduating, two babies as a sort of sabbatical, getting your teachers' training and perhaps a divorce while they're still toddlers and then all starting school together?'

I'm sure she intended a reproof, but she spoke very kindly. I looked at her slack old body in her slack old cardigan, her thatch of grey bobbed hair. She seemed to be preoccupied too. 'Is it the better way?' she asked again, gently.

'Yes, I think so,' I said. My marriage might have been ill-fated, but at least I had Dora and Toby. It seemed worth trying to get everything.

She smiled at me for the first time, a smile of great sweetness, as though I'd given the right answer at last.

'Well, it will be exciting to see how it all turns out, won't it; sink or swim.'

'It will,' I said.

I got up, realizing that I was being dismissed.

'Au revoir,' she said, 'I've put you down for Junior School Mathematics. I think you'll enjoy it.'

So within ten days of my husband's disappearance I was well on the way to starting a new life for myself. In retrospect it seems very sudden. (Of course, not as sudden as flinging oneself out of a window which I believe has been done by other wives similarly deserted.) The truth is that those ten days seemed an age. Carole's new baby, and other incidentals, certainly brightened the odd hour for me, but by and large the days (and nights) passed slowly, one pulsing minute after the other, so that no decision seemed sudden, but agonizingly drawn out.

The day after I saw Miss Hammond, Dora re-started Nursery School. It was the morning Victor had asked me to start work for him. I wondered if he had marked the date. I had a sudden sharp longing for him but it was soon sunk and lost in the morass of self-pity I was experiencing.

Mrs Wright, the head of Dora's school, had refused quite adamantly and I thought unfairly and rather tactlessly to have Toby even for two mornings a week; thereby refuting the firmly-held conviction on the estate that she would do anything for money. 'Not until he's two-and-a-half,' she'd said in her breathy, little-girl voice which we all imitated, sometimes working it in with the Yugoslavian accent of the clinic nurse. 'Darling, I can't make an exception.' This, when I knew very well that she had made one for Judy Wilson's Abigail. 'But he's two-and-a-quarter.' 'Yes, well, in another three months he may be ready for us, but not yet, I'm quite sure. I've got his name down for January, haven't I?'

Perhaps it was just as well. It was rather a formal school and Toby wasn't fond of sitting down or painting or listening to stories – though he liked books, which he usually held upside down. What Toby really enjoyed was moving things about from place to place in his cart, being very busy and his own boss. He wasn't usually noisy or destructive, but it must be admitted that he wasn't easy to organize.

And of course it was well known that Sheila Wright liked girls best, particularly dainty little girls, like Dora, who liked to dress up and sing and dance. We mothers were often submitted to an action song when we fetched our children, eleven or twelve girls dancing lightly on their toes, this way, that way, suddenly blown together like leaves in the wind, and six or seven unwilling boys in a separate circle who after several canters round, unaccountably changing directions a few times, finally heaved one another to the centre to clap hands or smite one another on the chest; they sang different words from time to time but the choreography remained more or less the same.

(To be honest, I never visualized Toby with either lot of dancers but with the smaller group of naughties who, encouraged by their mothers' presence, pranced about making faces and sick-noises on the periphery of the circles.)

'I mean, Toby's not as naughty as Justin Cole and Alexander Green, is he?' I'd asked Dora on the way home from seeing Mrs Wright.

'No, he's not,' Dora had said, and choosing her words with her usual care, had added, 'Mrs Wright is just a fat old bumnit.'

I think it was that evening that John's mother phoned. After I'd chatted a bit about Dora and Toby, how Dora had dolled herself up with my eyeshadow, how Toby had got his foot stuck under the pedal of his jeep, she'd suddenly asked for John and I'd had to say that he was out.

'Out again?'

'I'm afraid so.'

'When will he be back?'

'I'm not certain. I'll ask him to give you a ring when he comes.'

'That's just what you said on Sunday. Is he away?'

'He is at the moment, yes.'

'Is he coming back?' she asked then, after the briefest of pauses.

'I don't know. I hope so.'

'I hope so too,' she said then. 'Oh, I do hope so.'

She had never considered me good enough for John, I was too frivolous and unambitious; she'd never made a secret of it. Yet she seemed heart-broken that there was trouble between us.

'You were so good to him when I was there. He was behaving so badly and you were so kind. He's hard and moody like me and you were kind like Dad; Dad was so good to me.'

I knew she was crying. I'd hardly been mature enough to sympathize with her when John's father had died five years earlier. Now I could really feel for her. I considered asking her to come to stay, but my instinct for self-preservation was stronger than my altruism. I'd never found her hard, though she was certainly moody, but what would have daunted me were the endless sad reminiscences; all the pointless, boring details of things past would have been too much for me in my depressed state.

Dora, being young and resilient, was thrown in instead.

'Don't forget you've promised Dora she can come and stay with you during her half-term,' I said.

'Does she want to come?'

'She certainly does. She's going to cook for you.'

I felt that she was drying her eyes.

'I don't suppose she'll like it here,' she said, sniffing a little.

'I'll keep in touch,' I said as the pips went, 'I'll let you know.'

I really couldn't have done with her.

I could have done with my father, though, but I knew he wouldn't stay long. He was so easy, so understanding, so helpful. He washed up and cleaned with an absorbed thoroughness; he'd always done a lot in the house, possibly because my mother hadn't. He did the shopping carefully, going from shop to shop for loose bananas and special offers; he played with the children, though not so much as to make me feel guilty.

However, he needed my mother. In the ten days he stayed with me after she left, he seemed to shrink almost visibly. Perhaps it was my low state that caused it, but I honestly think that it was missing my mother. There are good marriages, my mother and father had one, they needed each other like actors and audience. I didn't talk much to my father, at least, not of my problems. He liked to talk about my mother, his mother and father and his elder and favourite daughter, my sister Barbara, in that order.

But I did talk, nightly, to my Samaritan, and wondered if I'd ever manage to do without him. After the first time, I tried not to keep him to myself for longer than five minutes. He was invariably courteous and interested, and though I sometimes thought he was dropping off – I always phoned him after eleven when my father had gone to bed – he invariably commented on any new piece of information, however trivial. He always approved of what I'd done.

Once in a while, as a change from trying to untangle my problems, I fantasized a little about him, our relationship had something of the Daddy-Long-Legs motif about it. Perhaps he just sounded old and sleepy, he was really perhaps a dynamic forty-year-old with lots of money and socialist tendencies. Once in a while, oh mercy me, I tried to be smart like Judy (née Jerusha) in her letters and had to pull myself up sharp; suicide and despair is what this organization deals in, I had to tell myself, it's not a marriage bureau.

Occasionally I even thought about marriage bureaux. In the event of my marriage ending in divorce, I would certainly consider one. Or the Personal Column in the *New Statesman*. (At no time did I envisage the possibility of remaining single, I don't know whether that says more about my nature or my upbringing, but life without a mate seemed insupportable, and the mate I wanted was a full-time husbandly sort.) Vivacious, warm, honey-blonde divorcée, mother of two, wants . . . There I got stuck. I wasn't sure what I wanted. Men were so difficult and unpredictable; they drank and swore and snored and made other body noises, they were lecherous and unfaithful. The more I thought about men in general, the more I wanted John back. At least I was used to his faults, and he had many good qualities; I listed them sadly.

I find it strange to think how little I considered Victor; someone for Friday nights just wasn't what I wanted.

It was Hugh Trent, John's boss at the BBC, who gave me news of him at last. He phoned one afternoon saying he'd received a doctor's certificate from John and a letter saying that he was suffering from severe depression and would be unfit for work for at least a month. He'd been attending a clinic every morning for the last few days and felt it was doing him some good.

'There's a message for you,' Hugh said then, and I gripped the phone and felt my legs buckle under me. I can't take it, I told myself.

'He asked me to get in touch with you,' Hugh went on. 'He feels ashamed that he hasn't himself, he told me to tell you that he will as soon as he feels able to.'

Hugh was plainly embarrassed by the situation. He said there was no address on the letter but offered to give me the address on the doctor's form. I said I would like it and wrote it down: 56 Harmsworth Road, W.12. My handwriting was spiked and shaky, hardly recognizable.

He asked me whether there was anything he could do to help. He told me to phone him (or Marilyn, of course) if ever I wanted a chat. Could I come over to see them? I would be more than welcome. As he talked, I stared at the address I'd written down. W.12. That was Shepherd's Bush, wasn't it? What was he doing there?

I let him try to comfort me for another moment or two, then I thanked him and he rang off.

Altogether, the situation wasn't so different from one of the many I'd thought of, but getting confirmation of the cold estrangement I'd been preparing myself for was numbing. I went upstairs and lay on the bed shivering and weak with the shock of knowing that he was hiding from me, that he intended to get in touch with me when he felt able to, as though I was a sort of monster that he would confront when he felt strong again.

Luckily the children were out with my father so that for a while I was able to hide away in bed, crying and moaning and banging my head about on the pillow.

I felt better afterwards. I changed my dress and put on fresh make-up and the lantern earrings Dora had bought me for my birthday. At least John was alive – I'd never really believed otherwise – and was concerned about me. I straightened the bed and went downstairs.

My Samaritan had asked me on one occasion whether I particularly minded the thought of John's lover being a man and I'd said it made no difference to me. I now realized that it did make a difference, somehow I found it a little easier to bear. There was something Grecian, exotic, immature, about the notion of his having a homosexual affair; I didn't feel so threatened by it; being so heterosexual myself, I couldn't see it having a permanent effect on our marriage. I was able to tell myself that his breakdown was the result of his failure to prevent the suicide and not the sense of loss.

Somehow I managed to comfort myself and was relatively composed when my father and the children came home.

While the children watched *Jackanory* I told my father about the phone call. He was so relieved to hear that John was safe that he immediately started making plans to leave me. He was certain that everything would now be well.

Chapter 14

The day after my father's return was another bad one. By the morning post, I received written confirmation of my acceptance for the one-year post-graduate teachers' training course. I should have experienced a slight sense of achievement about it, I suppose, but felt nothing but a tightening of the stomach. Included with the letter was a list of books for the Junior School Mathematics course, not one hinting at future pleasure or even composure. Most of them had titles like *New Concepts in Number Work* or even worse, *The New Mathematics*, making me realize that the coolness I'd always felt for the old mathematics had changed to affectionate nostalgia; hanging about at the children's playground later on in the day, I went through my tables; seven times, eight times, nine times.

To return to the morning; Dora wouldn't get up, wouldn't wash, wouldn't dress, didn't want to go to Nursery School. She listed her grievances: the paint was too runny, the jigsaws mixed up, the milk tasted of cardboard, Pauline May pushed in front of her in hand-washing and Simon Eliot was rude in the lavatories. She cried over breakfast, and though I told myself that it was still only the beginning of her term and that she'd be all right by the time I started at college, I wasn't convinced.

I'd arranged for Elizabeth to take her to school, but since she was so upset, had to take her myself and stay on until almost ten. When I finally got Toby to Margaret Flaxman, the neighbour who'd agreed to look after him for the college term, it was eleven and her young daughter was already having her nap, so I took him home again. I wondered if Margaret would have enough patience with him, she'd confessed to slapping him the previous day. She'd said it was because he had bitten Felicity, which I'd accepted at the time, but now I wondered about it, he normally only bit people he liked and he certainly wasn't fond of Felicity who was a large girl with a flat, vacant face like a rag doll. 'Did you bite Felicity?' I asked him as I took him home. 'Oh no,' he said, but he brightened up as though at some pleasant memory. Perhaps he had.

I was worried about leaving him and spent the rest of the morning examining my motives for doing the course. Was I really so desperate to become self-supporting? Now that I knew John was safe, I could surely depend on his providing for us? I had to admit that to a large extent I was simply making a gesture of protest at the way he'd walked out on us, which didn't seem worth the upset it was causing. I made myself feel thoroughly guilty and miserable so that I couldn't even face lunch.

The rest of the day was not much better. In the children's playground Dora fell from a swing and Toby threw sand at everyone near him even when I threatened to smack him and afterwards when I had.

Carole had promised to come to tea but failed to get Timothy ready in time; when she phoned at half past four she was still on the three o'clock feed. Children's television had an offering for the younger viewers on both channels which Toby scorned (even at two, sex and violence was what he enjoyed) so that I had to play trains with him until bedtime.

When I'd finally got them both to bed I was exhausted and demoralized. I had my eggs on toast and prepared myself for a lonely evening; I knew no one would call, people were almost as embarrassed by John's disappearance as they would have been by his sudden death.

There was nothing worth watching on television, I couldn't concentrate on a book, I knew a drink would only make me feel more sorry for myself. When the phone rang I rushed to answer it, feeling that it had to be something worthwhile. When I found it was a wrong number, I could hardly believe it; it seemed the last straw and monstrously unfair, as though everything was conspiring against me.

I suddenly thought of the purple hearts in the zipped hold-all on Dora's wardrobe. I'd never taken drugs but I knew they were fairly harmless, the things teenagers took for a lift, and my God, I needed a lift. The previous Sunday I'd been reading an article about sixteen-year-olds who regularly bought a supply on a Friday to take them through the weekend; I thought hard about it and decided to take one or perhaps two to help me through *Play for Today*.

Dora had a night-light in her room so that I was able to get at the bag without disturbing her. I pulled it towards me so that I could unzip it without any noise. It seemed heavy.

It was locked. I started to tremble. Somebody had been into the house. It was certainly locked, it had on it a small bright padlock I'd never seen before. I took the bag outside to the landing where I had a better light, but I was so unnerved that I had to go back to Dora's room. The bag contained far more than it had before, it wasn't heavy but seemed about a third full. I was really frightened. Too frightened to phone my Samaritan or my father or anyone – the police? I just sat on the edge of Dora's bed, drawing what comfort I could from her nice soapy smell and her steady breathing. Who could have broken in again?

The explanation, when it occurred to me, was quite simple. John must have let himself in while we were out, either that day or some time earlier. He had presumably decided on the old hold-all as the unlikeliest place for me to discover whatever it was he wanted to leave. What could it be?

After deciding that the intruder was John, I was no longer quite as alarmed as before and after about five minutes felt sufficiently composed to go downstairs.

What could he be wanting to keep locked away? More drugs? I didn't know what to make of it, and it didn't seem fair that I had to be trying to make anything of it. I walked about looking for signs of John's presence in the house, but could find none. I looked in his desk and in the cloakroom but nothing seemed to have been moved or taken away. I was still too agitated to sit still.

One of the things I'd recently discovered was how nervous I was in the house by myself, how much strange noises disturbed me: footsteps late at night, a car driving past when

I was almost asleep. I'd had to accept the unpleasant truth that I was, fundamentally, a very anxious, timid person, and this last episode certainly confirmed it. I walked about fretfully.

Well, I'd just have to get over the foolish state of nerves, that's all. I had no guarantee that John was ever coming back, and I couldn't bear to think of becoming the sort of person who double-locked doors and windows and looked under beds and behind curtains. How could I cure myself? And soon.

There was a sudden clatter from outside, someone dropping a bin lid, I think, and I found myself clutching the back of the armchair. It was ludicrous and pathetic and crazy. I didn't know whether to laugh or cry.

Then I had an idea of beautiful simplicity: I would get a dog. I couldn't think why I hadn't thought of it before.

John wasn't as fond of dogs as I was; had always maintained, perfectly reasonably, that a pet was something two people had to be enthusiastic about. But now the position was quite changed and if he did come back I was sure he'd understand how much I'd needed one. My God, I needed one. I'd feel safe with a dog in the house. I imagined myself standing at the door, my hand on its faithful old head. I imagined it curled up at my feet, growling slightly at the least noise.

The very next day I'd ring every pet shop and breeder in the area. What sort of dog was I after? I'd go into it thoroughly. I'd go to the reference library and discover what breed was the most suitable for life in a small house with young children. Of course it would have to be reasonably cheap to buy and not too expensive to feed. A licence cost little enough. A cardboard box would do for a bed with one of Toby's old blankets to line it. We'd call it Rover. Or Dog Toby. We'd take great trouble over its training. There had been some tips on *Blue Peter*; kindness and firmness. Heel, boy. Sit.

At last I sat down, feeling relatively happy and relaxed.

As I picked up the newspaper, my eye was transfixed by a small advertisement. 'Two-year-old mongrel bitch must have new home, owner emigrating.' I shot to my feet again.

The telephone number was a London one, but I would have rung anywhere; I felt I was meant to. My grandmother used to open her Bible at random, looking for a message; I'd got one, unsought, from *The Times* Personal Column.

'Yes, you're lucky, she's still available.' A woman's voice, sounding rather like an answering machine. Could she please describe her? She was white, affectionate, lively, and would eat practically anything. Well, medium-sized. She wasn't actually hers, but her brother's, but she would deliver her personally since he was in the country. No, they wanted no money. A good house-dog? She certainly barked a lot, though she couldn't honestly describe her as fierce. Yes, she'd bring her straight away. She'd be glad to.

The way she accepted the news that I lived at the far side of Bromley should have warned me, but didn't. I was far too excited. I cleaned the sitting-room and the kitchen while I waited, and started on the stairs. At about eleven o'clock, the doorbell rang and I could hear a nice, deep barking. A huge white dog bounded in as I opened the door. Medium-sized! Anyone describing her as medium-sized couldn't have been thinking of dogs, but of animals in general; cows, horses and so on. 'She's very big,' I said.

'Her name's Daisy. Her mother was a pedigree Dalmatian who was shown at Crufts. Shall I bring in her bed?'

I nodded dumbly. Daisy didn't have a single Dalmatian spot, only a pale fawn smudge over one eye. She was looking at me in a placid and friendly way. What could her father have been?

The woman was younger than she'd sounded on the phone, about twenty-two. She looked very Crufts herself; suède and cashmere and knitted stockings.

I fetched Daisy a bowl of water. She stood like a calf in the kitchen and drank it in three or four slurps. Her tongue was the same bright pink as our front door, Dulux geranium.

The girl came back with Daisy's bed, a wooden structure slightly larger than Toby's cot, though not as high. It had a cot mattress in it. She hovered at the door of the kitchen wondering where she could find room to put it down.

'It's a very small house,' I said, which was another way of saying that Daisy was a very large dog.

'You do like her?'

I hesitated over the next bit. 'Do you think this house is too small for her?'

'Oh, no.'

'I've got two children as well.'

'She loves children. She really is a supah dog. She has absolutely no vices. I'd have her myself like a shot, except that I only have a bed-sittah in Town and of course I work all day. I think in heah, don't you?'

'Yes.' It had to be the sitting-room. Our kitchen, 'carefully designed for maximum efficiency', certainly had no room for dogs – or even hamsters for that matter. She put the bed down in the children's play area between the settee and the armchair. Daisy came in from the kitchen and put her nose under the mattress, throwing it up. I thought she wanted to go home, to take up her bed and walk.

'That's her little game. When she does that she's asking you to put one of her toys underneath and she gets it for you. Good gal, Daisy.'

I put a blue rubber bone under the mattress and, sure enough, she fetched it and brought it to me. It wasn't brilliant but I was rather touched at the way she laid it at my feet, thudding her great tail.

'By the way, she's had her dinnah.'

'What does she eat?'

'Absolutely anything. Heart, mince, haddock, steak, you name it.'

'Will she eat tinned food?'

There was a slight pause. 'Oh, I should think so.'

I wondered why they were getting rid of Daisy. I certainly didn't believe in the brother who was emigrating, brothers of girls like this one didn't emigrate.

'Where is your brother going?' I asked.

'Gosh, is that the time. I must dash. She may whine a bit when you go upstairs, but it'll only be for the first few nights. You do like her? Look, my name's Amanda Drew. I'll give

131

you a tinkle tomorrow morning at about eleven. If you're not perfectly, perfectly happy with her, I'll come out to fetch her back tomorrow night. Will that suit you?'

'I'd appreciate that. Thank you. I'll be in all day.'

I certainly felt much happier. I was only, after all, taking her on approval.

'If you have any real trouble tonight, just carry her mattress upstairs. She'll sleep like a lamb if she has company. Oh, there's one thing, she's nervous of thundah. Most dogs are of course, only . . . most dogs, you know . . . hide under a table or something, but Daisy likes to sit on you. I thought I ought to mention it so that you're not taken unawares because she is rather heaveh. Anyway, perhaps we won't have any more thundah this yeah.'

Amanda went towards the door and so did Daisy. 'Sit,' Amanda said, pointing to the bed.

She slipped out into the hall and I followed her. I put on the outside light and saw her long red sports car.

'You do like her?'

'Oh, I do.' (I did.)

'I'll phone you tomorrow morning.'

I went back into the sitting-room and Daisy greeted me as though I'd been on a journey. 'Bed,' I said in Amanda's voice and it worked. I locked up.

'Come on,' I said, and she was up again and at my side. I picked up her mattress and carried it upstairs, which would have been easy if she hadn't been intent on thanking me on every stair. I put her mattress in my bedroom and straightened her blanket over it. 'Bed,' I said again. I went to the bathroom.

I passed the hold-all on the landing and pushed it to one side. I no longer cared what was in it.

When I got back to the bedroom, Daisy rushed past me and padded downstairs. I followed her, expecting goodness knows what trouble. She pushed her way into the kitchen and went to stand by the back door, turning to look at me. She didn't even whine. She really was a supah dog.

For ten minutes I stood at the back door in my cotton nightie while she explored every square inch of the garden before finally selecting the spot which smelt and looked and smelt again exactly right for her purpose. Ten more seconds and she pushed past me into the house and upstairs. She slept all night without stirring.

Dora liked her and so did Toby.
　'What is it, Toby?' I asked.
　'Dog,' he said.
　'He calls all animals dogs,' Dora said. 'Is it a dog?'
　'Yes. Her name's Daisy.'
　'Mummy, is she ours?'
　'Yes, she's ours.'

Amanda didn't give me a tinkle either that morning or any other. Daisy was certainly ours.

I'm not claiming to have discovered any universal cure for a man's desertion; I'm only saying that getting a dog certainly helped me. For a start, it completely disorganizes the old routine, there's little opportunity to brood when you have to do everything in half the time so that the rest may be devoted to long walks. Toby became so exhausted by playing hunt-the-slipper in the garden – at the time he and Daisy were at exactly the same hundred-and-one-times stage – that for the first time in his life he let me sleep until eight o'clock every morning. Dora became so intent on taking Daisy for her early-morning run round the estate that she jumped into any clothes I put out for her. We forsook all our old enemies at the children's playground and made interesting new friends in Queen's Park, including a military-looking gentleman with two Irish setters who said I – or Daisy, he was looking at us both – looked like his mother.
　The Vet became another friend. I couldn't understand how he could be so patient with us, about the uneatable things Daisy ate and other habits not mentioned by Spock, until I got his bill in January.
　Even my parents were happier about us, though my father worried about our having to leave Daisy alone when I went

to college. 'I've even got that organized,' I told him. 'Pam's au pair loves her and is going to take her out every afternoon.' (Eva was a large, blonde fraulein who used to walk five or six miles every day with Pam's two-year-old on her shoulders.)

My Samaritan, too, was very pleased. He was another dog-lover. The night Daisy came, I forgot to phone him and afterwards phoned only every other night, then every third night, and our chats became mere chronicles of dog days. I felt I oughtn't to ring him any more, but he said, why not, he wasn't busy. September was always a slack month, he said, and anyway I cheered him up.

About four days after Daisy came, we had to leave her alone in the house for an afternoon. I realized it was too soon, but I simply had to get autumn clothes for the children and shoes for myself and a birthday present for one of Dora's friends. So, having carefully removed all small, chewable objects, we left her in the sitting-room with a bowl of water and her own toys.

When we got back, she seemed fine, knocking the children over in greeting and pinning me against the wall to lick my face. Dora had bought her a yellow ball in Woolworth's, so as soon as I could I turned the three of them out into the garden with it while I made tea.

I found that she'd managed to push open the door from the sitting-room into the hall. However, since all the bedrooms and even the cloakroom had been left tightly shut, it didn't seem to matter. It had been much better than I'd expected, the sitting-room was completely unharmed.

I didn't discover the hold-all until I was putting Toby to bed. While he was playing in the bath and I fetching his clean pyjamas from the airing-cupboard, I saw it in the recess where I'd left it a few days earlier.

Daisy seemed to have taken it apart at the seams, indeed one end piece was completely missing. I could see bundles of letters inside and typed manuscripts, most of them chewed a little at the corners, some of them hideously masticated, nothing but a pulpy mess. I picked out some of the less slimy letters and recognized John's writing. I presumed they were things he'd appropriated, probably quite legally, from his friend's flat.

I was about to read one of the typed sheets of paper, when I remembered the purple hearts. At first I was convinced that Daisy had had them all and my heart thumped as I wondered how to break it to the Vet, but after a thorough search I came across them in a side pocket where Daisy hadn't reached.

My relief was so great that I found I didn't care too much about the devastation. I carried the bag and deposited it in the far corner of my wardrobe which I locked, and went back to the bathroom to find Toby out of the bath and dusting himself with Vim.

Chapter 15

On September 26th, the actual day before I was due to start at the college, I had another phone call from John's boss, Hugh Trent.

After a few preliminaries; how was I, how were the children, were they back at school, too young for school, of course he'd forgotten how young they were, well, they were company at home weren't they, and I was to believe him that they were easier at that stage than at any other; he told me that John was in hospital. 'Try not to worry,' he said in a calm, flat voice which made me realize at once that he was seriously ill.

He'd been operated on for a perforated ulcer a couple of days before, he'd asked Hugh to let me know where he was.

'They phoned me yesterday and I managed to slip in to see him last night. He wants you to go to see him, Tessa.'

'When?'

'I imagine he'd like to see you as soon as possible. Could you manage to go this evening?'

I sat perfectly still on the telephone table, trying to assess how I felt. It was like probing a tooth when the pain seems, improbably, to have stopped.

'Yes, I could manage it,' I said at last. 'But are you sure it wouldn't be too soon?'

'What do you mean "too soon"?' Hugh asked obtusely. He was obtuse, but not to that extent.

'Hugh, did he suggest my visiting him, or did you?'

'He did, Tessa. Honestly. He asked me whether I'd been in touch with you and how you'd seemed. I said you appeared to be coping admirably with everything and he went on about what a frightful time you must have had and how guilty he felt, and I took the liberty of saying that I was sure you perfectly understood. I said that you had always struck me, Tessa, and Marilyn is in total agreement with me on this, as a sympathetic, liberal-minded person who'd be more than willing to help a person through a crisis.'

He waited a moment, as though hoping for confirmation of his touching faith in me. Since it wasn't forthcoming, he continued, 'So I think the ball's in your court now, Tessa. Do you feel you could go along tonight? Do you have anyone to look after the offspring? I'd suggest that Marilyn come along except that she's not terribly well this year.'

'Yes, I'll go tonight.'

I wrote down the address of the hospital, the number of the ward, the visiting times.

It was a quarter past eleven when I went into the kitchen to make myself some coffee. Toby was in bed, Dora at Nursery School, Daisy in the garden. I'd been trying to clean the whole house before the beginning of term. I'd finished the upstairs; bedrooms and the bathroom, all the windows, and was cleaning the stairs when the phone had rung. I decided I wouldn't do any more. While the kettle was boiling I got the Hoover from the stairs. I was interested to note that I was exactly half-way down. It seemed significant, a statement of my life; half-way. That's how far I got with everything. Half married, half deserted or half free, depending on one's point of view.

I let Daisy in, wondering why I wasn't happy. John had asked me to go to see him. He was ill and needed care and attention. I'd get the chance to tell him I wanted to start again. Did I want to? Of course I did. Surely I did. Only I was half prepared for college and a new way of life. I suddenly crumbled up the biscuit I was giving Daisy and handed her a fistful of crumbs which she blew over the floor, looking at me sadly. Daisy, Daisy, give me your answer do. I kissed her on the top of her head and scratched her between the ears, but when she realized that no other biscuit was being offered her she went to lie on the settee without a backward glance. I flung one at her. Sometimes I thought her a mistake.

I got Toby up and we fetched Dora. 'Why have you been crying?' she said, accusingly. 'I hate it when you cry.'

In the afternoon I phoned Pam to ask her whether Eva was free to baby-sit, she was, and then Carole to ask her whether

Walter would run me to the station for the six-fifty train, she was sure he would. I told Carole about John's operation and how he'd phoned to ask for me. She told me how her uncle had died of a perforated ulcer.

'How's Timothy?' I asked.

'Not too well. The Health Visitor came this morning and said I wasn't to give him any baby rice or Farlene or soup, nothing but Cow and Gate.'

'But you're not giving him anything but Cow and Gate.'

'I know. And I'm not to.'

'But that's wonderful. He must be getting on awfully well if you haven't got to supplement.'

'I knew you'd say that, Tessa. You're like Walter, you have this need to be cheerful about everything. Last night he was a terrible colour, absolutely waxen, but of course Walter had to say he'd never seen him look better. I was so worried I didn't sleep all night. Then after the six o'clock feed when I did doze off, he went to work without saying goodbye or good luck or anything, and he knew the Health Visitor was coming at eleven this morning.'

'Do you think Timothy's coming between you?' I asked gravely, but she didn't answer. 'I must go to the nappies, Tessa,' she said, as though they were all crying for her, 'I'll tell Walt.'

In another two weeks, unless the real mother had a change of heart, Timothy would be legally theirs. She'd surely relax when they'd got it in writing.

For the rest of the day I was too busy to think much, but in the train up, with the evening paper Walter had kindly bought me on my knee, I suddenly realized what an important decision I had in front of me; teachers' training and independence or, if John wanted it, loving wife. That was it, I'd do what John wanted. I wasn't free. It made it easier in a way.

To my surprise John's mother was in the hospital entrance waiting for me. (He had phoned his boss and his mother but not his wife, a further indication, if I needed any other, of how things stood between us.)

'Thank goodness you've come, Tessa,' she said – she was looking old and tired – 'he wouldn't let me phone you before. Everything will be all right now, won't it?'

'How is he?'

'He's very weak, but he'll be all right now. It seems a good hospital.'

'You'll be coming home with me tonight, of course?'

'Oh yes, I'll stay till he's better. I'll be able to look after the children while you visit. I'll be a help to you, won't I?'

She took me to the men's surgical ward. John was in a small private room at the top of the ward.

I hardly recognized him. He was in hospital pyjamas, thick flannelette ones, green and white, the sort old men wear. His face was very pale and thinner than ever. There was a plastic tube in his nostril and his mouth was slightly open. He was asleep, or at least his eyes were closed. I found I was clutching my mother-in-law's arm.

'Sit down,' we said to each other. We sat on the two hard chairs by the bedside and listened to his shallow breathing.

'No wonder he was out of sorts,' my mother-in-law said.

I said nothing. We sat, straight and still and silent, for several minutes.

'I'm supposed to be starting a teachers' training course tomorrow,' I said then.

I thought perhaps she hadn't heard me, we were both talking in whispers, but I could tell by her face that she had. I waited for her to comment, but she didn't.

'How are the children?'

'Fine.'

We sat in silence for another minute or so.

'We've got a dog.'

Again there was no comment, only a slight tightening of the mouth.

'I was nervous by myself.'

'I would have come.'

'She's lovely. The children are mad about her.'

'Will John like her?'

'I'm sure he will. If he comes back.'

'Of course he'll come back. There's no question of anything else.'

'How do you know? Has he said anything?'

'Of course not. What would he say to me?'

'He left home. I haven't heard a word from him for over three weeks.'

'He was desperately ill.'

'I would have nursed him.'

'People turn against those nearest to them sometimes. Frank didn't want me at the end, the doctor said it's often like that.'

She took out a handkerchief. 'Don't be hard on him,' she said, dabbing her cheeks.

'Of course I won't. If he wants to come home, I'll be very glad, of course I will. But I'm not sure he will want to. You see, it wasn't only his illness, there was another person involved.'

'Nonsense.'

We became aware at the same moment that John had opened his eyes and was looking at us. I smiled at him. He said my name very quietly but didn't smile.

'A drink?' his mother asked him.

He nodded his head. She fetched the glass of water and raised his head so that he could take a few sips. 'That's all,' she said. 'Shall I sponge your face?'

He nodded again. Afterwards she turned his pillow and straightened his top sheet.

I was sorry that her husband had turned against her at the end. I hadn't heard that before.

A staff nurse came in then, and asked us to leave because the doctor was coming in to see him again.

'Do you want me to come tomorrow?' I asked him, looking into his eyes, measuring the slight pause before he replied.

'If you can, please.'

'Is there anything you'd like me to bring you?'

'Books.'

'Pyjamas,' my mother-in-law said. 'I'll buy you some nice new pyjamas.'

'Knit me some,' he said, but without smiling.

We both stood close to him to say good night, but he had closed his eyes again. We had to go, then.

'You must have a word with Sister,' my mother-in-law said. 'Her room's just up here.'

'You have a word with her,' I said. I had to rush towards one of the chairs in the corridor. After a time, a young nurse brought me a drink of water. I don't usually mind hospitals but that was different; that visit.

The Sister told my mother-in-law that John's condition was satisfactory and she repeated the word angrily all the way in the Tube. 'Satisfactory, indeed.'

We were lucky to catch a fast train back.

My mother-in-law slumped into the corner of the empty compartment and shut her eyes. She looked exhausted. She had no one but John and he wasn't kind to her; he liked her well enough but forgot about her most of the time. She slept for a few minutes but woke with a start at London Bridge.

'Have we arrived?'

'No, not yet. Another twenty minutes. Close your eyes again.'

'No.' She sat up and adjusted her hat and her chiffon scarf. 'I won't sleep tonight if I drop off now. I wake so early as it is, not a minute after five.'

'You go to bed too early.'

'No, I don't. I go to bed same time as I always have, but I can't sleep after five. Most older people are the same. I think it's the sins of our past lives that wake us up, perhaps good people sleep till eight.'

'A couple of days with Toby and you'll sleep till eight,' I told her. 'Sins, indeed.' Please, please, don't let me cry, I prayed to no one in particular. Those days I cried so easily. 'When did you leave home? Yesterday?'

'No, last week, a week today.'

'Has he been in hospital as long as that?'

'No, he phoned me to say he was ill. I begged him to ring you. He said he had contacted you but that he didn't want to go home just yet. So what could I do but get the next train to Euston and rush to this flat in Shepherd's Bush where he was staying. And it was lucky he had the sense to call me, he was in a terrible state.'

'All I'd heard was that his boss had had a doctor's certificate saying he was suffering from depression. That's all I'd heard.'

'He collapsed in the bathroom on Friday morning. I had to ring 999 to get the door down. He was rushed to hospital and they'd operated within the hour. Depression indeed. They'll say anything these days to save making a proper examination.'

'I can't understand . . .'

'I can't either. I suppose it was the children getting on top of him; him being so ill they would seem boisterous. He said he went home one afternoon, early on; a few days after he left home.'

'Yes, I knew he'd been. He left some things.'

'I don't know. He said he'd been. Perhaps he intended to stay, I don't know. He said your parents were there, I suppose that made him feel awkward, to know they knew about it. And you were out. Oh, I'm not trying to make excuses for him. It's beyond me what's got into him. You know I didn't want him to get married so young. I didn't make any secret of it, but once you were married, I tried to help all I could, didn't I? Once married, you have to make the best of it, that's what I always say. He's got everything, that's what I kept on telling him; two beautiful children, good job, lovely house, central heating, nice wife; everything to live for. It's just the ulcer that got him down, I'm sure of it, just that old ulcer. It made him melancholy. No wonder the doctor thought it was depressions. Frank used to be the same with his stomach. Every spring he used to get the depressions; Frank, I used to say, we've got everything in the world to make us happy; the pension, free passes on the buses, a good library, all the books you've never had time to read . . .'

I only half listened. I wondered what she would say if she knew about Adam Beauchamp whom John had loved as he had never loved me.

I was seized by doubts. Now that I'd seen John again I was less sure that I wanted to save our marriage single-handed. I just wasn't in command of my life. I'd made an honest effort to become independent, I'd got a place in college, I'd managed to get a grant, I'd made satisfactory arrangements for Dora and Toby, and I was going to give it all up – I realized I was – without even knowing whether my husband wanted to resume living with me. Since he'd left me I'd been thinking of him as he was when I first knew him, and of our marriage as a precious, living thing. Seeing him again had only made me realize that we were different and separate and apart.

When we got home, Daisy gave me her usual boisterous welcome but was gentle and subdued towards my mother-in-law, as though realizing that she was tired, worried and not altogether won over by large white dogs.

Eva said the children had been marvellous; Toby had been awake and wanting playing all night, he was marvellous, Dora had gone to sleep like a little angel, she was marvellous, and the cheese pie was marvellous, she had eaten it all. And Mrs Meadows had phoned. It was urgent I went over to see her if I got back. Of course she would stay to give my mother-in-law a cup of tea and what a pity she had finished the marvellous pie.

Rather wearily I went to Carole's. I'd already been summoned for hiccups, diarrhoea, prolonged hiccups, sickness and projectile vomit; goodness knows what other crisis awaited me.

Walter opened the door with a self-conscious smile.

'How's John?' I told him but he didn't seem too interested. He took me into the sitting-room. Carole had Timothy with her on the new G-plan settee. It couldn't be too bad.

'What's the matter now?'

'He's smiling,' she said, in a flat, tragic voice.

'It's a bloomin' stupid thing to get you round for, Tessa,' Walter said.

'He's only four weeks and three days,' Carole said. 'Please don't say it's wind. Six weeks it says in my books, six to eight weeks. Come and stand here, Tessa, you'll see.'

She held Timothy close to her and clicked her tongue at him. She smiled at him. She nodded her head at him. She made several noises like uncorking a bottle. He looked vaguely in her direction, a well-fed, slightly cross-eyed, blank look.

'Let me have him,' Walt said.

'Hold his head.'

'Woo, woo, woo,' Walter said, like a man unused to that particular form of address. Over his shoulder, Carole made train noises. 'Woo, woo,' Walt said.

'Let me have him.'

'Hold his head.'

I went through my considerable repertoire of baby talk while Timothy looked gravely at a spot just to the right of my chin.

'Don't call us, we'll call you,' Carole said, taking him from me. And he focused his plum-coloured eyes at her and smiled. It was a nice moment.

Before I went to bed I wrote to Miss Hammond, the principal of the East London and Kent Teachers' Training College, explaining to her why I would not be attending the course after all. I felt sorry not to be seeing her again.

After my mother-in-law had gone to bed, I phoned my Samaritan. As usual he didn't say much, only listened to me.

'And I don't know even now whether he wants to come back. I don't even know whether I want him to. I suppose I do. I suppose that would be the best thing. I've got to look after him for a time, anyway. That's all I'm sure about at the moment.'

'That's it. Just take it from one day to the next, that's the best way.'

That night I dreamed about Victor. I was rushing somewhere, in a desperate hurry I seemed to be, it seemed vital that I should arrive in time. I was running up escalators, through long corridors, just getting on to trains as they left, running across dangerous roads, at last arriving at what seemed to be my destination. I remember going through a revolving door and up a short flight of steps and into a huge brass lift. I was about to press the button when I saw that there was a uniformed attendant in the lift and it was Victor. I said I wanted the top floor and he pressed the lift button and after a bit he held my hand – at which I wasn't surprised. He opened the lift door and let go my hand and as I looked back he was smiling tenderly at me so that I knew he didn't want me to go, but I had to go, and as I looked back I saw the door of the lift closing and I was on my own and there were no doors at all on the top floor, and when I went back to the lift, there was no lift, and no way up nor down.

I woke up then and cried. My dream seemed more terrible than anything. Victor had come back to me and I had lost him yet again. I could hardly believe it was only a dream, it seemed so real. I had to get out of bed and pace about. I wondered if my mother-in-law was awake. It was just gone five o'clock.

Chapter 16

The next day, I cancelled the arrangements I'd made for Toby and cut Dora's attendance at Nursery School to three mornings a week, as it was before, and arranged my days around hospital visiting. Victor was back in my mind again but I didn't let him obtrude. The situation hadn't altered; my duty was to John and the family.

My mother-in-law seemed particularly quiet and withdrawn. I found myself, on occasions, inviting the often-repeated stories. 'Tell Dora,' I would say, 'about the time you took John to the Science Museum and what he said to his teacher the next day,' and Dora would look at me with widened eyes, whispering in the kitchen afterwards, 'Do me a favour!' her favourite catch-phrase at that time.

John got stronger, day by day. At first we talked very little, I was maternal towards him, turning his pillows, straightening his sheets, rearranging the things in his locker so that everything was to hand, telling him cheerful little anecdotes about Dora and Toby. For the first three nights this worked very well because after about ten, fifteen, twenty minutes he would sink back on his pillows closing his eyes, probably feigning sleep so that I should be still and quiet. So that for the rest of the visiting hour I would be still and quiet, creeping out when the bell released me.

The fourth evening, he was obviously a great deal better. The tube had been removed from his nose and he was sitting up in bed in the main ward.

'You're late,' he said. He held out his hands to me and kissed my cheek. He pulled up the chair so that when I sat I was very near him.

'Toby squirted some of my perfume into his eye,' I started to say, but he stopped me.

'How do you feel about me?' he asked.

146

I was thrown, and unable to answer truthfully. (I don't think I could have answered truthfully in any case.) I hedged and prevaricated.

'John, what do you mean? You know how I feel about you, nothing's changed as far as I'm concerned . . . What do you feel about me, isn't that more to the point? After all . . .'

'All right, I deserve that. I'll ask you a simpler question. How do you feel about my coming home?'

'I'll be very pleased, delighted, when you come home, of course I will. I was desperately upset and worried when you went. Have you any idea when you will be coming home?'

'Next week, I think.'

'You'll be pleased to be out of here, particularly now that you're in this ward.'

'Yes, it's pretty awful. It's the first time I've even been in hospital. Have you ever been in hospital?'

'Only with Dora. Do you remember the Sister of the ward I was in? Do you remember how upset I was when you were late visiting? Gosh, and how thrilled when you were first one evening. Isn't it strange how little things seem so important? It's the same for poor Dora at Nursery School, she hates it when I'm late. And yet she doesn't want me to be first, I suppose that makes her feel conspicuous. "Be the second mummy," she's always saying. It's quite difficult to arrange.'

Back with the children I felt safe again. How did I feel about John? I'd agonized enough when he disappeared. I looked at him and wondered about it.

As a child I'd once seen a chicken running about with its head cut off. I often thought about it. I thought of it now. I had the cold calm feeling, like a small stone dropping into a still, grey sea, that the anguish I'd felt for John was the nerves reacting after the body's death.

'Whatever's the matter?' John asked. 'What *can* it matter whether you arrive second or last? She knows you'll come. You're obsessed by trivialities.'

'I suppose I am.'

'No, you're not. You're a very good, conscientious mother and I'm a monster to be impatient with you.'

He lay back on his pillows and looked at me affectionately, so affectionately that I shook off my post-mortal fancies and took the opportunity to break the news about Daisy, telling him how nervous I'd been on my own. 'I hope you won't mind her,' I said. 'I'll try not to. I hope she's not one of those small, yapping dogs.' 'Oh no, she's not.'

I didn't ask him that evening or on any other where he'd gone on the night of the barbecue, or why, or why he'd found it so difficult to get in touch with me directly. I expected him to tell me some time, but he didn't. Not of his own accord.

On the night before he was due to come home, he seemed in excellent spirits. He said he'd been able to do some work during the day; he'd had an idea for a series of programmes for sixth-formers, had phoned Hugh Trent who'd been enthusiastic, and had done some preliminary planning. He'd written out a list of books he wanted me to get for him from the library. He seemed his old self; more normal than he'd been for at least six months.

He reached for my hand. 'Isn't it wonderful,' he said, 'to be suddenly excited about work again, to be filled with enthusiasm? Even though my private life is in such a mess.'

I think he realized immediately that he'd gone too far. Perhaps I'd flinched a little.

'God, I'm sorry,' he said. 'I shouldn't have said that.'

'Yes, I think you should have. I think it's time for us to be honest with each other. Perhaps you should start by telling me about your private life; why it's in such a mess. I really think you should.'

'I know I should. I owe it to you, Tessa, I know that. Look, I'll tell you everything, all the sordid details, and you shall decide what I'm to do. I'll leave it to you, you've been so good and patient.'

To my surprise his eyes were full of tears, so that I almost took pity on him. One part of me wanted to be magnanimous, to suggest that we postpone the talk until he was stronger, but the other part was simply dying with curiosity, and after a moment's struggle the worser part won.

'Tell me about Adam Beauchamp,' I said.

John lay back on his pillows. I think he had expected compassion.

'He was her husband,' he said.

'Her husband?' My mind, turning a quick somersault, strove for equilibrium. 'Whose husband?'

'Didn't you know she was married? She married straight out of school, when she was eighteen. They weren't living together, of course. She was getting a divorce. How did you know anything about Adam Beauchamp, though? Who told you about Adam Beauchamp?'

'The police came.'

'What about?'

'Don't you know he committed suicide?'

'Of course I know that. That's why I had to rush out that night. She was desperate, absolutely desperate. She'd got it into her head it was her fault.'

'Was it?'

He gave me a very cool look. 'Of course not. How can you ask such a thing? He was a suicidal maniac, everyone knew that. He'd been in and out of mental hospitals for nearly two years. She'd had an impossible time with him, any other person would have gone under, he was a bloody maniac. But what did the police come to us about?'

'He'd left a letter for you with our things.'

'What things?'

'The things that were stolen from our house. He'd taken them.'

'He'd taken them?'

'Didn't you know?'

'Of course I didn't know. Our things? My transistor. Good God, he was quite mad, you can see it now, can't you. Breaking into our house. All that havoc he left. I thought it was a gang; three or four men.'

'What did he want?'

'How the hell do I know what he wanted. He must have got hold of my address from somewhere. Perhaps he thought she was living with me. It must have been that. He thought she was living with me.'

John was quiet; absorbed in that thought, I suppose.

'I thought he might have been after the purple hearts in the bag in Dora's room.'

'Good God, Tessa, whatever made you think of that? As though he'd go out to Bromley for a few purple hearts, even if he knew about them; you can get them anywhere. Whatever have you been reading? You really are very naïve, Tessa.'

'I thought perhaps he hadn't got any money.'

'He'd got masses of money.'

'He left you a letter. Didn't she tell you about the letter? She must have known about it.'

'I haven't seen her since that weekend. I stayed with her and looked after her that night and the Sunday, but on the Monday she went to her parents in Scotland. I put her on the plane at Heathrow. She said she'd be back at the end of the week.'

'So you stayed on waiting for her to come back?'

'Yes, that's it, waiting for her to come back. I know I should have phoned you, I was going to, I just wanted a sign from her first.'

'Didn't she get in touch with you at all?'

'No. Of course, she was in a state of intense shock.'

So was I. All my carefully worked-out theories dashed. I could hardly rally my thoughts.

'I felt so sure the purple hearts had something to do with it.'

'For God's sake, Tessa, don't go on about the bloody purple hearts. Giles Armstrong left those when we put him up for a couple of nights when he was trying for that job at King's.'

'You didn't mention them.'

'I wish to God I had. I just thought you'd worry about them. So I put them in that bag in case he called back for them, and he never did.'

'Why didn't you post them to him?'

'Why should I? Why should I risk getting into trouble?'

'What risk would there be?'

'Damn, they are illegal, aren't they?'

'Then why risk keeping them in the house? In Dora's room, too.'

'It was foolish, I admit it. Tomorrow, I'll flush them down the lavatory. They're really on your mind, aren't they?'

There was a long silence during which I contemplated the interesting conversation I'd have with my Samaritan later on.

'It'll be nice to have you home,' I said at last.

'It'll be nice to be home.'

'I suppose you'll stay until she summons you again.'

'Tessa. Oh, Tessa, I can only promise you this; I'll always tell you everything from now on. I'll always be deeply ashamed of rushing out the way I did without leaving you a word of explanation. I can only say that I wasn't myself. I was driven wild by the fear that she would commit suicide as well; she mentioned it, she said she couldn't get the idea out of her mind. That's all I can say, I was possessed by fear.'

I felt his fear. His upper lip was wet with it as he talked.

'Afterwards I fell ill. That's all I've got to say. I've told you everything. I don't expect ever to see her again. She only needed me for that period of crisis.'

'Do you think you'll get over her?' I asked, quite gently. I felt I had the right to know.

'I think so,' he said, but sounding very doubtful.

On the way back in the train, I tried to get to grips with the different story. It wasn't easy. Believing John to be homosexual had soothed my pride, had made his rejection of me less insulting; I wasn't as ready to accommodate the barefooted dancer again – if it was she – and I wasn't going to risk any other guesses.

At least one thing now made sense, my mother-in-law's reluctance to let me fetch the newish, grey gaberdine mackintosh she'd left in the flat at Shepherd's Bush where she'd been looking after John. I'd offered to get it before going to the hospital, it was fairly near, but she'd begged me not to, had become really agitated about it. She'd obviously been told or had sensed that the flat belonged to John's girl-friend and was afraid I'd find out. I wondered how much she knew. She pretended to believe that there was no one else involved, that John's leaving home was due entirely to his illness, but I knew she couldn't really think so, she was too perceptive where John was concerned, she watched him too closely, he was all she had. She knew, I was sure of that.

She was in her dressing-gown when I got back, she liked to be in bed before ten. I told her how well John had seemed that night.

'I think I'll go home the day after tomorrow,' she said. 'I'll just wait to see him back and then I'll go.'

'Oh, I hoped you'd stay a week or two at least. It would be such a help. You'd be able to keep the children out of his way a bit.'

'They'll do him good.' She sounded rather harsh.

I felt she was being tactful, that she feared to be in the way of the reunited couple, so I increased the pressure.

'He'll be feeling very weak at first. I'll have to take the children and Daisy out in the afternoons. Will he be well enough to be left on his own?'

'I'm sure he will. You baby him too much. Try not to worry so much about him, Tessa.' She left me and went into the kitchen.

It wasn't the sort of advice I'd expected. 'Don't worry so much about him.' The world seemed to be turned upside-down, it wasn't just me.

She brought in the sandwiches she'd made and our milk drinks.

'I'm thinking of getting married again,' she said.

I stirred my Bournvita carefully and looked at her, but I could see that it was my turn to speak. 'How very exciting,' I said.

'Exciting indeed! A widow of sixty-four, and a widower sixty-nine. Very exciting.'

'Oh, come on, it is. Do tell me about it. Please.'

152

She suddenly relaxed in her chair and I realized how seldom she did; usually she sat upright as though waiting and listening.

'He lives up the road, he always has, but I've only recently got to know him, not that I know him all that well. I went to the Over Sixties once or twice with Mrs Morland; he goes most days. He brings me my paper now, it saves me paying delivery. He goes down most days. He likes walking. He used to be a postman, though not our way.'

'When will you get married?'

'Oh, nothing's been said yet. I'd decided against it really, till John was so ill. I mentioned it to John when I was down in July but he advised me not to, he said I was comfortable on my own and indeed I am, I've got everything I need. Only, having someone in the house is much more practical when you're older; for instance, if you're not too well one day.'

'Of course it is.'

'I'm not saying there's anything to him, not really. Now Frank was a reader and a thinker, that's who John got his brains from, as well you know, and that makes a man very easy to live with, because all he needs is his books and his papers. Harry is more a practical man, he likes to walk and he's got an allotment, but he doesn't say much. Well, neither did Frank, there's nothing much to say when you've been married thirty years, but Harry just stands about, it gets on my nerves sometimes. Usually he just leaves the paper and perhaps a cabbage, but if I ever say, "Come in a minute," I'm always sorry, because when he's had his cup of tea he just gets up and stands about and looks at me and waits for me to tell him to go. He never takes any initiative.'

'He asked you to marry him.'

'Yes, but he doesn't ask for an answer. He told me to think about it but that was nearly four months ago and he's never mentioned it since.'

'It's a good thing he didn't; you might have refused him.'

'He hasn't got his own house and I have.'

I thought of her small neat semi; pretty, because she'd never been able to afford the embossed nylon carpet and the three-piece suite and the wrought-iron magazine rack and matching mirror that her neighbours had, or had simply had the good taste to stick to the mahogany sideboard and round table and bentwood chairs and the large comfortable armchairs she'd had when she got married. She'd lived in the same house since 1932.

'You wouldn't want two houses,' I said.

'He'd be getting more out of it than I would, he'll be able to save on his rent, though perhaps he gets Supplementary for that, I don't know. He's got one of the little terrace houses at the top of the street by the bus-stop, I wouldn't want to move there. I don't really know what to do. In a way it's nice to be on your own, though I miss Frank terribly. You don't have to plan anything or cook if you don't want to. Of course, I never had Frank at home all day, so I'm not used to it. No man will make do with a boiled egg for dinner. On the other hand, the shopping will be much easier. I hate asking for a quarter of this and two ounces of that and would they mind cutting it in half.'

I was finding it difficult to follow her reasoning for and against, but was delighted that she seemed so animated, usually she went in for long, dreary recitals about John's scholastic career from when he started at St Edmund's Primary at four-and-a-half, no, four-and-three-quarters, to when Dr Simon, head of King Edward's, had said he couldn't take German and Latin for A-level and how Frank had gone to the school and been invited to rearrange the time-table, and had.

'Sometimes I'd do anything in the world for a cup of tea in bed,' she said, 'but what really decided me was John collapsing in the bathroom; who'd know or care if I collapsed in the bathroom?'

'When will you tell him?' I asked her.

'He calls for the paper money on a Friday morning, so I'll ask him in for a cup of tea, and perhaps bring it up, perhaps not. He's very kind. And not just to me, he does go out of his way to help people. He's got that on his side; he is kind, I will say that.'

'And when do you think you'll get married?'

'One thing I know, it'll be me who'll have to decide it all, and arrange everything, I know that. I do feel he's a bit of a stranger. He's done odd jobs for me though, he fixed a washer in the scullery and just before Easter he replaced that pane of glass above the front door; it had been cracked for years. John won't like it at all, he'll think I'm marrying beneath me, but there you are, I don't like everything John does, but it doesn't stop him, does it?'

She knew all right whose flat he'd been living in. I was filled with tenderness for her, partly because I felt she liked me and felt concerned about me, partly because she'd roused herself from the apathy she'd let herself be engulfed in for the last five years and was thinking of remarriage; it really was quite courageous.

Colette talks of the courage, the absurd courage, of young girls when they get married; all in all, the courage of an elderly woman seems even more remarkable, even more absurd. She knows the odds, her eyes aren't dazzled. She knows how petty and irritating are a man's habits, she knows his faults, laziness or meanness or conceit, as well as she knows her own. It seems so much to be taking on when all you want in return is the occasional cup of tea in bed and to be able to buy butter by the half pound. And a bit more, perhaps.

'Let's drink to it,' I said, getting out the gin and two glasses.

'Here's to your happiness,' I said, but it was to her courage I was drinking.

'He's a nice figure of a man,' she said, 'I will say that.'

Chapter 17

When Dora heard that John was coming out of hospital, she was unwilling to go to school, and though he wasn't coming until the afternoon I let her stay home to help get everything ready.

She dusted the sitting-room and polished the dining-room table and carried all her toys into my room (I was putting John in her room; I knew he would be pleased by the arrangement and I wasn't really concerned about it), and then made fairy-cakes by adding an egg and a tablespoonful of water to some bright yellow powder from a packet, discoursing, at the same time, on her favourite subject: death.

'What would happen to me if you had to go to hospital?'

'Daddy would look after you, or Grandma.'

'Or Granpa and Granma Hardiman.'

'That's right.'

'They may all be dead.'

'They won't *all* be dead, there'll be *someone* left to look after you.'

'What if they all be dead?'

'Then Auntie Barbara would look after you.'

'And Uncle David?'

'That's right.'

'Is Auntie Barbara your sister?'

'Yes, my big sister.'

'She's not as big as you. You're *much* bigger than Auntie Barbara. Shall I eat the rest of this?'

'Yes, all right.'

'It doesn't taste very nice, a bit like poster paints. Hasn't she been planted?'

'Who?'

'Auntie Barbara.'

'Planted?'

'With seeds. *You know.*'

156

'Ah . . . well, the thing is, I don't think she's very keen to have a baby just yet. She's a lecturer at a University.'

'Is that important?'

'Yes, it is.'

'She'd probably be too important to look after me.'

'I don't think so.'

'What if you *die* in hospital?'

'Dora, I'm not going to hospital. And in any case I'm not going to die till I'm a hundred, I tell you that every night.'

'It's not very long to a hundred.'

'You know it is. Please don't make me count now, it's so boring and we must take Daisy out.'

'It's not very long to a hundred.'

'But, love, every number you say is a whole year, one birthday right through to the next, so it's very, very long.'

'I don't like Uncle David.'

'Oh, I do. He's very kind and very funny. Do you remember the time he . . .'

'He's probably not a good planter. Can you remember being planted?'

'Oh, look, here's Grandma and Toby.'

'I hope we don't have to have Toby till a hundred.'

I'm sure any psychologist would jump to the conclusion that Dora was morbidly inclined at this time because John had so suddenly disappeared from her life. He would be wrong. She had been the same for well over a year. The nursery rhyme she always wanted was 'Who Killed Cock Robin?', insisting on all the verses and of course soon having them by heart. 'Who caught his blood?' she used to recite to Toby with melancholy fervour; 'I, said the Fish, With my little dish, I caught his blood. Who'll make his shroud? I, said the Beetle, With my thread and needle, I'll make his shroud.'

I can't account for it; she certainly didn't get it from me. For me, my father had to bowdlerize and alter extensively because otherwise I cried and couldn't sleep. So the old woman who lived in the shoe finished off by kissing all her children soundly and putting them to bed, and Old Mother Hubbard, finding no bone for her dog, hurries off to the Baker Man to get him a cake as fast as she can, and Peter Rabbit's father was put in a cage by Mrs McGregor. (It was only on reading the book to Dora, twenty years later, that I discovered the horrible truth concerning the pie.)

Perhaps all small children are preoccupied by death and disaster, and that the stronger, like Dora, confront the monsters, while the weaker, like me, try to hide from them.

'We saw Carole,' my mother-in-law said. 'Dear, dear, she is a tiring girl, isn't she? She thinks you've turned against her and I wouldn't blame you if you had.'

'Oh Lord, I forgot to ask her how she'd got on at the clinic.'

'I've never seen an all-white pram before. Beautiful, isn't it? Nice enough little baby, too. I had to examine his finger-nails and listen to his breathing. She only let me come away because Toby coughed.'

John came home by ambulance. He was tired after the journey but he stayed downstairs for about half an hour. He seemed happy to be home. Daisy greeted him exuberantly as though he'd been long-lost, and even Toby's eyes lit up, though that may have been at Dora's cakes, decorated with whorls of synthetic cream and scatterings of hundreds-and-thousands.

'Everything is all right now,' my mother-in-law said when he'd gone to bed. 'He's his old self, isn't he. Did you see how thrilled he was to see Toby? He loves them, doesn't he. He's like Frank about that. Frank loved kiddies, it was such a pity he never saw his own little grandchildren, wouldn't he have spoiled them. He could never say no to kiddies. I remember Mrs Ifield who lived in No. 22 saying, "You're better than a mother's help, Mr Jilks, the way you take them off my hands." He used to take Tracey and Wayne down the park every Sunday morning till they moved to Leicester, and never brought them back without ice-cream or a packet of crisps. They still send me a Christmas card, fair play. The kiddies must be teenagers by now. Don't tell him what I told you about a *certain person*, will you? Not until I've gone.'

She went home the next day and John and I settled down to another interlude together. It was rather like our holiday in Devon, we were on our best behaviour, anxious that things should go smoothly. John didn't seem to mind Daisy too much; he could see she kept Toby happy in the garden for long periods every morning, and he was probably glad of the peace in the afternoons when we took her for her walk.

A fortnight after John's return from hospital, we had his boss and his wife to dinner. Hugh Trent is a large, fleshy, handsome man preoccupied with food and drink and women in that order, and since I'd cooked an elaborate meal, had in plenty of booze and was wearing a dress with a spectacular cleavage, he seemed happy and the evening went well.

His wife, Marilyn, is tall and thin with a sad, almost haunted look. She reminds me of the ladies who stand looking out to sea or contemplating a church in Victorian problem pictures. Her face is so expressive, yet no one seems to know what her story is. I think about her even when I don't see her for months; she's somehow not a negative person; she rarely talks, but her glances are often extraordinarily penetrating. She has traces of beauty, though not the type, one would have thought, to have appealed to Hugh.

Once, at a party, I saw an exceptionally handsome young man take one of her hands in his, stroke it, examining it carefully, thoroughly. 'No one, not even the rain, has such small hands,' he said in a tender, devoted voice, and I found myself hoping fervently that he was in love with her, that they were having an affair; but the next thing he said, in quite a different voice, was, 'God, what a bore the reorganization of Sam Naylor's department is going to be,' and proceeded to tell her all about it. It was a let-down for me, but her expression remained exactly the same. I stopped eavesdropping at that point.

Hugh generally ignores her, though he talks about her a great deal in her absence as other men talk of their mortgages.

At about midnight, after listening politely for hours, though contributing little; intellectual people like Hugh always talk about Fulham and nude shows and bull-fighting; I settled down to think about Victor. The wine had left me pleasantly muzzy and it brought back to me, very clearly indeed, the way I'd felt after the brandy on Midsummer Night and after the large quantity of incredibly cheap wine on the night of the barbecue. Mahler's 'Das Lied von der Erde' had finished and I put on the Beatles record they'd played over and over at the barbecue, and which I'd bought the previous week. John seemed a little surprised, but Hugh said, 'Ah, real music at last,' – he would – and I withdrew my attention, as Marilyn had done over the soup.

'I love you,' Victor said, disturbing me because I realized that he'd never said it to me in real life. Or had he? I had the feeling that he might have, on the night of the barbecue. I strove to remember; it suddenly seemed of the greatest importance.

'You look sad,' Marilyn said.

'It's this song.' I had to say something, because tears were suddenly falling over me; great drops like thunder rain. I shook them away and hummed to the music.

Marilyn listened gravely until the end of the record.

'It's the school concert next Monday night,' she said in her quick, precise voice, which always seemed greatly at variance with the gentle look and Virginia Woolf hairstyle. 'Jeremy is in the orchestra, he's a flautist.'

'How old is he?' I asked, touched because she was trying to cheer me up.

'He'll be seventeen on New Year's Day.'

We smiled at each other like people exchanging intimate secrets.

'And Felix is nineteen.'

'Is he at University?' I asked. I knew he was.

She nodded and seemed about to speak again.

'These are our two.' I fetched the photograph from the window-sill. 'Dora and Toby. She's nearly five and he's two-and-a-bit. Toby doesn't really look like that, not always, any-way.'

After she had smiled and nodded, not wanting to be too much of a burden on her, I returned the photograph to its place and fiddled about with the curtains and changed the record, and when I sat down again, turned towards Hugh and John as though hearing something interesting from that direction.

They were talking about John's proposed series of programmes for sixth-formers, and in fact it was interesting enough to listen to. As far as I could make out, the programmes were taking the form of conversations between various poets, ancient and modern; their actual words, adapted only when absolutely necessary. In my opinion the device seemed artificial, even dangerous, but John and Hugh seemed to think it highly original and no one asked for my opinion.

It was a woman they called Lara Richardson who was writing the scripts and I had one of my intuitive flashes – which had so far had a hundred per cent failure rate – that she was John's girl-friend, the other woman, Adam Beauchamp's wife – or rather, widow.

'Is that Adam Beauchamp's wife?' I asked, a trifle humiliated at having the sort of intuitions which needed checking up on.

'Yes,' Hugh answered, with more than a hint of embarrassment, as though my asking the question was not quite the thing.

'Yes, that's right,' John said, giving me a small smile which seemed to bestow on me, if not his full confidence, at least enough to be going on with.

'A very dangerous woman, in my opinion,' Marilyn suddenly said from the small chair by the bookshelf where she was looking through a nineteenth-century photograph album.

Hugh and John both stared at her and she closed the album with a snap and seemed ready to elaborate.

'Good God, is that the time,' Hugh said, jumping up with uncharacteristic haste. 'We'll positively have to fly. We've had a really stimulating evening, haven't we, Marilyn?'

'I liked Adam Beauchamp,' Marilyn said in her distinct,

unworn voice. She rose from her chair looking at John, Hugh and me in turn. 'I liked him.'

'She's another nutter,' John said when they'd gone and we were clearing up. 'No wonder she liked Beauchamp, they were two of a kind. Two bloody psychopaths.' He was extremely upset.

'Go to bed,' I said, 'it's ridiculous that you're up at this time of night.'

He went to bed, and after I'd finished the dishes I had another drink and put the Beatles record on once more.

Next morning, John was cheerful again. When I took his breakfast tray upstairs he was already working at the improvised desk in Dora's room. He congratulated me on the meal I'd prepared the previous night.

'I'd like to read you a bit of this,' he said.

I leaned against the door and tried to feel pleased. Wasn't this what marriage was all about? Discussions about work; confidences shared, problems aired.

' "Call me Dylan." Isn't that an enchanting beginning?'

'Good enough for Herman Melville.'

'What exactly do you mean by that?'

' "Call me Ishmael." '

'OK, if you're in that mood.'

'I'm not in any mood. I've always loved that beginning; it's great. Even in the film it was great. Did you ever see the film? Look, I've got to rush now. Let me have a look at some more of it when I get back from taking Dora. I'll be as quick as I can. It certainly starts well.'

All the way to Nursery School, I was determined to be charitable. Why couldn't I ever be kind to John? He wasn't happy. His affair – if it had ever been an affair – was over, and his miserable obsession would work itself out of his system more completely if I let him alone. (Miserable obsession? Who was I to talk about miserable obsessions, as far as I knew the lovely and talented Lara Richardson was the love of his life.) 'Call me Dylan,' I kept on saying to myself savagely. It would all be pretentious and derivative rubbish, I was pretty sure of that, but it was Hugh Trent's job to tell him so, not mine. John was cheerful because he was working with something of hers which he hoped would bring them together; and if her work was as hopeless as I imagined, she would be likely to be extremely grateful to anyone who gave her the slightest encouragement. 'She's a dangerous woman,' Marilyn had said, the first opinion I'd ever heard her express about anyone, and Marilyn was no fool.

It was well after half past nine when we arrived at Nursery School but to my surprise – she usually ignored late-comers – Sheila Wright took me to one side. 'My dear, I was so sorry to hear.'

I said, 'Oh, well, everything's all right now. John's convalescing, getting better every day, he'll be back at work next month.'

'No, I mean about you.'

'What about me?'

She looked at me strangely. 'My dear,' she said, in her little-girl voice, 'aren't I supposed to know? Oh gosh, I do hope Dora hasn't been indiscreet.'

'What has she told you?'

'About your hysterectomy.'

'Dora told you that I was having a hysterectomy?'

'What she actually said was that you were having your womb out.'

'How strange. I'm not. I'm perfectly fit.'

'But you have to go into hospital?'

'No.'

'No?'

'I'm afraid she's got hospitals on the brain. I'm sorry.'

'But she was crying about it after break on Wednesday. I had to leave Mrs Brown to cope here and take her into the garden for a little chat. I was going to tell you about it then, but I missed you.'

'My mother-in-law's friend had a hysterectomy. I suppose she heard us talking about it.'

'And you're perfectly all right?'

163

'Yes, perfectly all right.'

'I must say, you look perfectly all right. Well. I feel a proper fool. I can usually tell in a minute when they're making things up, I can usually spot it a mile off. But she was actually crying, wondering whether you'd die and so on.'

'She does a lot of that.'

'Oh dear . . . Well, perhaps it's natural in a way. I mean, with your mother dying when you were on holiday; that must have been a terrific shock for you all.'

I shook my head and bit my lip. 'My mother's not dead.' I felt almost ashamed to belong to such a healthy family.

By this time the children were rushing about noisily from one room to another, a thing never allowed, some still in their outdoor shoes. The bad boys were actually playing Batman on the stairs; I could hear Toby's unmistakable 'Bap-ma!' as he flung himself about. I'd never heard such a healthy rumpus before, not even at their Christmas party.

'She described everything, even the cemetery overlooking the sea.'

'There was a cemetery overlooking the sea,' I said, as though this excused her, 'and a new grave with wreaths on it.'

'One in the shape of an open book – white roses and carnations?'

I shrugged my shoulders. I hadn't inspected them and wasn't aware that Dora had.

Sheila Wright turned to me again. 'Do you think I ought to mention it to her? Tell her I've found out that she's been telling me a pack of lies?'

'I think it would be better if I did. I don't think she realizes what she's doing.'

'I won't say anything, then.' She sounded rather disappointed.

She moved away from me and clapped her hands for silence and I picked up Toby and made my escape.

And as I untied her, Daisy, nervous or cross at being left so long at the gate-post, made her escape, so that we had to chase her right to the bottom of the avenue. Toby was so excited when we finally caught up with her, that he swallowed a prune stone which he must have had in his mouth since breakfast, so that I had to get him out of the pushchair and turn him upside down and thump him, to the horror of two elderly ladies on their way to the shops.

He started to roar then, not because of any pain or indignity but because I refused to give him back the prune stone, and then to cry and sob in a heart-broken way, saying he wanted to play Batman, he didn't want to come home with me – the elderly ladies turned back, nudging each other – so that I had to take him to the stationer's on the corner to buy him a Matchbox car, and since they only had the more expensive kind I didn't have enough money left to buy the fish for John's lunch, which would mean another trip to the shops later on.

It was still only ten o'clock, but I felt decidedly worn, and the more I thought about reading Lara Richardson's script and being kind, the less kind I felt, so instead I went round to Carole's. I hadn't seen her for a week.

Chapter 18

He was theirs. Timothy Walter Meadows, son and heir; the papers had arrived the previous day.

'Why didn't you let me know?' I asked, because the best defence is attack and I could tell she was offended by my neglect.

'I didn't think you'd be interested.'

I gave her a long, hurt look.

We shut Daisy and Toby in the kitchen with the new car and two biscuits each and settled down in the sitting-room with a jar of Nescafé and a kettle.

'He's being christened on the sixth of next month. Will you be able to come?'

'Rather.'

'Will John be well enough to look after Dora and Toby, do you think?'

'When is it? A week next Sunday? Yes, I'm sure he will. No problem.'

'He won't be offended if I don't ask him and the children?'

'Of course not.'

'You see, I've got twenty-two people and the house is so small. Lesley's are making the christening cake, I've just been phoning them; I can't decide whether to have it completely white with "Timothy" written in silver, or the other model with blue and white roses round the edges and a white cradle as a centrepiece; that's more expensive.'

'Then I'd get that.'

'Why?'

'Well, I mean, I wouldn't, but I think you should or you'll only worry because you haven't got the best.'

'I suppose you're right. Walt always says . . .'

'That you get what you pay for.'

'That you get what you . . . Yes. That's what Walt always

says. All the same, I think I'd like "Timothy" written in the centre.'

'Have that and the cradle. I can't see it would be difficult. Be rash.'

'I wish I'd thought of that. I'll ring them again. No, I'll get Walter to ring them, he'll be able to explain it better than I will . . . There are ten other babies being christened on the same afternoon, I think that's pretty shabby, don't you? It seems to be mass-production for everything these days. Walter's spoken to the vicar but it's not within his power to arrange anything different, so I suppose we'll have to go along with it. I hope you aren't offended about not being asked to be godmother.'

'Heavens no. I hadn't even thought of it. Gosh.'

'Are you sure?'

'Absolutely.'

'I would have liked you to be godmother but the thing is, a boy only has one and I think Evelyn would be rather offended if she wasn't asked, don't you?'

'Yes, I do.' (Evelyn was Carole's much older half-sister, a teacher at a girl's school on the south coast.)

'I think you're disappointed, all the same.'

'I'm not. I hadn't thought of it. Honestly.'

'I thought of it. You've been a good friend to me, Tessa, but as Walt says, you're not really religious, are you?'

'Not really.'

'Not at all. I mean you *never* go to church, do you? And, after all, if the service isn't to be a complete mockery, you have to consider things like that.'

Being asked to be Timothy's godmother had certainly never crossed my mind. All the same, I did start feeling a little offended, particularly since my candidateship had apparently been vetoed by old Walt.

'My grandfather was a vicar,' I said.

'I know. I told Walt that.'

'And my great-uncle was a rural dean. My father's family were all very religious, very high church, too.'

'You are hurt. Oh, dear. Now I can't ask you what I was

167

going to ask you.'

'Whether I'll stay home from the service and get the tea ready.'

Carole said nothing but looked embarrassed so that I relented. 'Of course I will, you idiot. I'd prefer it. I haven't got the clothes for being a godmother; I bet Evelyn's got a hat.'

'Oh yes. And a turquoise suit with a mink collar.'

'Perfect.'

'Victor is going to be one of the godfathers.'

I thought about that for a minute. Of course, I should have guessed it.

'Then I'm afraid I won't be able to come, Carole. I'm sorry.'

'Why not, Tessa?' She looked at me pathetically, as though being punished for something she hadn't done. 'Why ever not?'

'I'm sorry. I'm terribly sorry, I really am.'

I was too miserable to say anything more. Luckily, she realized how serious I was and didn't try to dissuade me.

'I'd better go now, Carole. John wants me to read some awful script for him.'

I fetched Daisy and Toby and the new car.

'Thank you for the coffee.'

She saw me out.

'I know about you and Victor,' she said at the door.

'Then you see why I can't come.'

'No, I don't.'

'Because it's over. Didn't he tell you that?'

'No.'

'And I mustn't see him.'

'I'm sure he expected to see you. Oh, do come in again and talk about it.'

But I went home. There was nothing I wanted to add; I was just too miserable about everything.

When I got back, John seemed to have changed his mind about wanting me to see the script – it was called 'Happy Ring

Time' I remember – and neither of us referred to it again.

Wanting to be well out of the way, I arranged an outing to the country for the afternoon of Timothy's christening. John was almost completely fit again and we were going to walk in the woods outside Sevenoaks and gather autumn leaves and seed-heads for the nature table in Dora's school and, although it was November, take a picnic tea.

We set out straight after dinner in brilliant sunshine. At first Daisy wouldn't get into the back of the car – John had only got it back from Shepherd's Bush a few days earlier and she'd obviously never been expected to squeeze into the back of a Mini before – but when I threatened to leave her behind, she got in quickly enough and behaved beautifully. We drove to Seal woods.

There were several families out walking and we collected admiring looks from everyone. The four of us were in identical Aran sweaters which my mother-in-law had spent all year knitting, and Daisy seemed the perfect dog for walks in the woods. How many people, I wondered, would be thinking of us as the ideal, television-advert family; John and Dora, dark and handsome, Toby and I, fair and bonny; he and she striding on in front, Toby and I falling behind; and the large, exuberant dog tearing from one couple to the other in an effort to look after us all. It was the last occasion that we were ever out together.

At about half past three it started to rain. There seemed to be no warning; we were drenched by the time we got back to the car.

Dora, rain dripping from her hair, was quite undaunted. 'Oh, please, Daddy, don't let's go home. Look, it's clearing up. I can see a little bit of blue sky. We must have our picnic, oh please, Mummy.'

I certainly didn't want to go home, but the sandwiches were wet and so was the blanket we were carrying, and Daisy, who had been plunging into the undergrowth instead of sheltering under the trees with the rest of us, was abysmally and miserably wet and kept shaking herself over us, so that it seemed the only possible thing to do.

All the way back, I was certain that we'd arrive exactly as Carole's guests were returning from church, but strangely enough I was spared that.

I changed the children's clothes and my own, dried their hair and mine, and then dried Daisy with a towel and a hair-dryer. Afterwards I put on the television and sat in front of it playing Lotto with the children and looking through the Sunday papers at the same time, but all I could think about was Victor over at Carole's without me.

John had gone upstairs and after a while I could hear him typing. I envied him; it seemed an engrossing occupation. I turned my attention to making tea. Most of the picnic tea was damp so I decided to make scones and afterwards perhaps fairy-cakes and chocolate-pops.

Dora came out to help me and as soon as the cowboy film was over Toby joined us as well and insisted on lending a hand or two. After the frightful rubbing-in process was finished, Dora rolled out the dough and Toby cut out rounds with a fluted pastry-cutter and I transferred several to the baking-tin and most of them back to another bowl for a re-run.

We'd got the first batch into the oven when John came down. 'Where's my hold-all?' he asked. 'The one that was on Dora's wardrobe?'

I hadn't consciously been keeping it from him, I'd simply forgotten all about it. 'Didn't I tell you that Daisy got it?' I said. 'I'm awfully sorry.'

Hearing her name, Daisy got up from her bed and came to lick my hand.

'Got it. What do you mean, got it?'

'I'm afraid she made rather a mess of it.'

'Where is it?'

'It's in my wardrobe, actually. In the corner of my wardrobe. I'll come up and dig it out for you.'

John followed me upstairs. So did Daisy.

'Why ever did you take it down from Dora's wardrobe? It was safe there.'

'I was going to have some purple hearts.'

'Whatever for?'

'I was miserable. And when I found it locked I was so frightened that I left it on the landing. I just couldn't think who'd been into the house. I told you about that in hospital, surely. Didn't I? Here it is.'

It looked worse than I remembered.

John sank down on to the floor in front of my wardrobe and started to examine the hold-all, feeling it with both hands, as though mere sight wasn't enough.

'It was the first time I'd left her,' I said gently, trying to divert his attention.

'Who? Left who?'

'Daisy.' Daisy, hearing her name, padded in from the landing and licked my hand again.

'It's no one's fault,' I said.

John took out a key from his trouser pocket and unlocked the padlock, though there was not much need, one side of the bag had been completely torn away.

He unzipped the top and took out some letters, not too badly damaged, and some thin folded manuscripts which seemed unscathed, then a thick manuscript, then many, many, completely chewed-up pages, some of which had ended up like great lumps of discarded papier maché.

'It's Lara's novel,' he said, after turning over every separate chewed-up fragment and lump. 'She asked me to read it.'

I bent down to pick up the undamaged part, intending to point out, I suppose, how much was still intact, but he snatched it from me.

'I've lost everything now,' he said. 'Absolutely everything.'

If he had knocked me about and kicked Daisy, I don't think I would have minded half as much as the way he sat in front of that bloody manuscript, fondling it and on the point of tears.

All the sympathy I had for him went. He'd completely forgotten the dreadful time I'd had when he'd simply disappeared and given me no sign that he was even alive. If I'd have come across him making love to a real girl in our bedroom, I don't think it would have angered me as much as to see him prostrate himself in front of that bloody bag of rubbish. If it wasn't rubbish, why wasn't it somewhere being published?

'Why the hell did you bring it here?'

He roused himself. My anger must have penetrated his stupor. 'I wanted it to be safe. She was in such a desperate mood – destroying everything.'

I wanted to say several hurtful things, but something stopped me; an awareness that there was tragedy somewhere behind this tour de farce. Poor Adam Beauchamp had committed suicide and Lara, whom Marilyn Trent had called, probably with justification, a dangerous woman, had been in a desperate mood, was perhaps still in need of help. It wasn't my problem but I suddenly felt sorry for everyone again, even for John.

'I was wrong to think we should stay together,' I said gently. 'I think you should go back to Lara.'

He shuddered with what might have been pain or joy. He said nothing for a time.

'She doesn't want me,' he said then. 'I don't think she wants me.'

'Neither do I,' I said. 'I want you to go. I don't mean immediately, of course. I mean when it suits you. When you're well enough. When you're able to arrange everything.'

I turned and left him, and Daisy padded downstairs at my heels.

While their parents' marriage was being torn apart, Dora and Toby had been most happily occupied; Dora rolling out a greyish lumpy mixture which Toby, a pastry-cutter in each hand, was stamping at haphazardly. 'Twenty-one,' he was saying, 'twenty-eight, twenty-two, bang bang.'

I was just in time to rescue the first batch of scones from the oven. They didn't look promising, but I spread butter and jam on them and swept all the rest of the pieces on to a baking-tin and into the oven for Daisy. Then I washed hands and faces, table and floor and made a pot of tea.

John came down and had a cup of tea with us. He and I

were both sad and talking was too much of an effort, but for my part I had no doubts about the course we were taking. And as for John, he didn't offer even a token resistance to the idea of leaving us. It was obviously what he wanted. I wondered that he had ever come back.

I admit that the thought of Victor being so close at hand saved me from the worst despair. I knew I was going to contact him quite soon.

Although I had no certainty then that the affair would be on again, that he still wanted it; I'd twice refused to see him and twice refused to talk to him on the telephone. And at that time I certainly didn't think of him as anything but a Friday-night date. Still, I had him at the back of my mind.

The wonderful thing was that I'd stopped thinking of a permanent relationship with a man as the only possible way of life for me. It had taken me months to reach the conclusion that many would have accepted at the first inkling of trouble : that I was better off without a man who didn't want me and whom I didn't truly want except as a status symbol.

If I were forty-five, instead of twenty-five, I suppose I might have had to try to mend the marriage, to salvage something of it, but all I could think of was the years of vigorous life I had in front of me and how I wasn't going to waste them. I suppose my attitude could be dismissed as completely selfish, but I still defend it. I still think any individual's first duty is to remain sane and as happy as possible. That poor mother throwing the crockery around and committing suicide in the television quartet I'd recently been watching, had made a profound impression on me. I felt I wasn't cut out to be a martyr. I never got the heroine's part even in the school dramatics. I just haven't the build for it perhaps.

The next morning, John managed to contact Lara – she had returned only the previous week from her parents in Scotland – and she agreed to his going back to live in her flat. He seemed keen to assure me that he hadn't found true love and security but only a stop-gap. 'Who ever finds more,' I said. At that point we were both very near tears.

173

He asked me to take the children out while he was packing and moving out. So I left Daisy with Eva and took them by train to London and gave them lots of treats; Underground trains and escalators and the Changing of the Guard and the ducks in St James's Park and lunch – Toby had a plain roll with tomato ketchup – in a Wimpy Bar. I expected to feel wretched and I did, as though there was a leaden weight on my stomach, but even so I knew it would lift before too long.

On the way back in the train I told them that John was going to live nearer his work but that he'd be coming to see them every week, bringing them *Pippin* and Smarties. Toby seemed quite satisfied, but I had to lay on a bit more for Dora; Zoos and visits to Grandma and Ballet.

Luckily the break came when Dora was completely wrapped up in me. It was later that she fell in love with John, and by that time she was used to the situation and quite enjoyed, I think, having him to herself. Toby was then, as always, pretty self-sufficient.

This is a poem I wrote about Toby at that time. It is not much of a poem, but it brings him alive for me, the boy he was then.

To My Son

Plod along your puzzled paths,
Hum your tuneless little songs,
Solemn, round-eyed, two year old,
Roar your great frustrated roars.

Monkey faces, gusty hugs,
Graceless movements, accidents,
Tumbling words, prolific tears,
Warmth as sweet as summer day.

May someone always, soon and late,
Turn at your coming and your going
Full of love, as now I do.

When I'd put the children to bed that night, I made plans for the future. I wrote yet again to Miss Hammond, principal of East London and Kent Training College. I realized, I said, that I had forfeited my place for the current year, but wondered if she would reconsider me, for the next. I told her that I'd regretfully come to the conclusion that I wouldn't make an enthusiastic or even efficient mathematics teacher, but that if she thought I might train to be a teacher of French, I would be most grateful to hear from her in due course. I even found and enclosed the testimonials – fairly good – which I'd received from my professors when I left University.

I phoned my parents, letting them know the latest developments. My father was worried and sad, my mother delighted. Nothing on earth will ever convince her that John was not a homosexual and while, as she said, she had nothing against homosexuals, she didn't think it much fun for her daughter to be married to one. She wanted me to promise to see a solicitor as soon as possible. (My father, on the other hand, wanted me to promise to do nothing in a hurry. I seem to remember promising both.) They were relieved when I said that I didn't want them to come up, and promised to spend Christmas with us.

I contacted my Samaritan in order to sign off. We had a long and pleasant conversation, the first for several weeks. I asked him whether it would be in order for him to come to tea, and he said he would like it very much and asked whether he might bring his wife. We arranged a Sunday. In the event, though, a letter arrived from him on the previous Thursday to say that he had developed an attack of bronchitis and would be unable to come. He didn't suggest another time nor did he ask me to phone again. Perhaps it wasn't in order, coming to tea. I think of him fondly. He was a very present help in time of trouble. Before the Samaritans were founded, people just had to pray, I suppose; a pretty lonely alternative.

Chapter 19

I rang Victor at his work exactly three days after John had left home.

It seems to show a most insensitive haste, but that's what I did. I wanted to see him, of course; wanted him. But almost as much, wanted to get John out of my mind. (It was the same for Gertrude, perhaps, posting with such dexterity to incestuous sheets. Why didn't she say as much to that male chauvinist son of hers, 'The hey-day in *whose* blood is tame?')

I rang him at his work. I asked for him and was told he was in conference. I was invited to give my name and did so. There was a moment's silence, then his voice, a little stiff and strange. 'Hallo, Tessa.'

'I'd like to see you,' I said.

There was a very slight pause, then he said, 'That's what I'd like, too.'

I said, 'Tomorrow night, then.'

He said, 'Fine.'

And that was it. And fine it was.

Though not immediately. At first he was hurt and angry that I'd rejected him so completely at a time when I was in trouble, furious for instance, when, somehow, I mentioned ringing the Samaritans.

For about two hours we sat together in his car, he'd got a new car which I rather resented, while he grilled me about every development of the last two months. You mean you were really frightened when you found stuff in the hold-all, really frightened? You mean, you thought I wouldn't be interested in the fact that you were frightened? But you didn't think it was my problem? Do I strike you as the sort of person who . . . ? Am I to understand . . . ? What exactly are you implying by . . . ? Then you must suppose . . . ? Do you honestly and truly believe . . . ?

He'd got glasses on, black, oval frames, he looked very different, stern and a little pompous.

We sat there, both of us, I knew it even at the time, desperately wanting to kiss and make up, but with every passing minute sitting more rigidly apart, until I couldn't quite see how we were going to. He was getting more and more pedantic and aloof.

It was a little like the complicated and ancient courting rituals of certain birds; I felt as though we were walking round and round each other, following an exact pattern, keeping a precise distance; every time he took off and put on his glasses I couldn't help thinking of rising plumes and feathers.

I wanted to cry, but was determined not to, because I was, after all, a newly independent woman and had to fight back. Tears would have been like submission.

'That's how it was, anyway,' I said at last, my voice as steel-cold as his, 'I've told you everything. There were several weeks when I couldn't bear to think about you.'

He let that sink in. There seemed to be a very long pause during which I was terribly nervous, then he clutched at my hand and squeezed it very hard. He was looking straight ahead and seemed to be in pain. I was certainly in pain, and when he loosened his grip I couldn't think of anything but of straightening out my fingers very slowly.

'I broke my toe when I was thirteen,' I said at last, because it didn't seem as though he was going to say anything ever again.

He kissed my fingers then and put his arm round me.

'How?' His voice was quite different. He took off his glasses and put them away.

'A horse stood on my foot.'

'Purposely?'

'Who can tell? I'd got my sister's boots on and they were too small for me and when I got one off to examine my blister, the horse side-stepped very neatly on to my toes. I never went riding after that.'

'You couldn't bear to think about me.' After another long

but less hostile silence, he took me in his arms. He hadn't driven to the Common, but at least it was dark.

'Victor, I was confused. After a while, I thought about you all the time.' He let me comfort him.

'What did you think about most?'

'Yes.'

'It's all you think about isn't it, as far as I'm concerned?'

'No. What's the matter?'

'Oh, I thought you meant, no.'

'No, I meant, no, that isn't all I think about.'

'Oh, it is. Well, what else do you think about? Do you ever think about spending the night with me, for instance, waking up with me, having breakfast with me?'

'Of course I do. All those things as well.'

'I don't know. I don't really know you at all. One night, several nights, I thought I could bear the separation if I'd had just one weekend with you, seen you asleep, cleaning your teeth, I'm sure you've never wanted to see me cleaning my teeth. Oh God, I haven't seen enough of you. And that first night, I thought I'd be able to give you up as soon as I'd had you. It wasn't as though I was looking for anything permanent or even important.'

'Don't sound so aggrieved.'

'I am a bit aggrieved, yes, I suppose I am. I've picked up girls before, without wanting to . . . well, I don't quite know what I want, but my God, I love you, I know that.'

I tried to sit up, to catch and savour the words I'd waited to hear, I didn't want them vying with the many other sensations I was experiencing at the same time, but it was too late, I couldn't, I simply had to let them go. I think he said, 'But my God, I love you, I know that.'

Later it certainly seemed as though he had. It was as though he'd proposed love and I'd accepted it.

He came home with me. I introduced him to Eva who was baby-sitting and to Daisy, who both gave him precisely the same dumb, adoring look, and afterwards took him to see the

178

sleeping children whom he examined very thoroughly, and then he made me a sandwich and put me to bed and let himself out with my key and let himself in with it before I was up the next day, and thereafter came to see me several times a week. I couldn't understand, then, how I'd ever made do with Friday nights.

On Boxing Day, we left the children with my parents and had three days on our own. We'd booked the bridal suite, a four-poster bed, in a small hotel in the Cotswolds.

For days beforehand, I'd kept on telling myself that it would turn out badly, that anything too long and longingly anticipated was inevitably doomed, that bliss wasn't a state given to human beings for the payment of a ten per cent deposit, that it would be an expensive let-down. I rehearsed every possible calamity so that nothing should take me by surprise; we'd be bored, cold, overtaken by doubts and scruples, laid low by food-poisoning or cystitis, we'd argue and quarrel (there must be something I cared about enough to argue over. Apartheid, child-prostitution?) I got into such a state that I was almost hoping that Dora or Toby would be slightly ill and so prevent our going.

However, they were completely fit and moreover in bed and asleep when he called for me at eight o'clock on the evening in question.

I introduced him to my parents, my mother was cordial, even a little sentimental, my father slightly hostile, though I hoped it would be apparent only to me. We left almost immediately, my mother telling Victor to drive carefully, my father telling him, rather mournfully, to take care of me.

'Your father doesn't like me at all,' Victor said, as soon as we got into the car. 'He thinks I'm a proper bastard.'

'This is how it's going to begin,' I said, 'the row we're going to have.'

'Are we going to have a row?'

I looked at him. He seemed, if anything, pleased about my father's hostility. 'I'd be just the same,' he said, 'if I was your father. Worse, probably.'

We stopped for a drink in one of the smart Thames-side villages just off the A4. The saloon bar was opulently decorated with Christmas bells and holly and tinsel, but in spite of that it was rather cold and almost empty. We sat as near as we could to the small fire and held hands. Because of the Christmas rush, we hadn't seen each other for almost a week and we seemed to realize it in the same instant and briefly our faces touched.

It was certainly only for a second. What we both wanted was to finish our drinks and to be on our way.

As we drew apart, the landlord was behind us.

'We don't want any of that,' he said, shaking his head a great deal.

At first, neither of us understood what he meant.

'You can go and do that somewhere else,' he said. He was about fifty with a big shaggy head and a large, white face.

I choked into my drink. I couldn't believe that he was taking exception to our chaste kiss. Afterwards I wasn't sure whether to giggle or explode, so I did a little of each.

'We will,' Victor said in a pleasant, level voice. 'Oh, we will.' We finished our drinks and stood up. He put his arm round me and kissed me again.

'It's my wife,' the landlord said as we left. 'It really upsets her, the kissy-kissy stuff. She can't bear it.'

I was dressed in a beautiful Edwardian cape, pale grey velour with black braiding, which my mother had got for me for Christmas at an antiques fair. Under it I had a cinnamon brown dress with a high neck and high boots. I was growing my hair, I've forgotten the exact stage it was at, but I have a distinct impression of tendrils. I thought I looked elegant.

'That awful man thought I was a tart,' I said, as soon as I'd got into the car. I was greatly affronted.

But Victor looked as gratified as though he'd pinned something on his chest. Loving him though I did, I could only describe his expression as smug.

In fact, he looked rather smug for the whole three days. And for another fact, the whole three days were perfect in every way.

The hotel was an old Elizabethan farmhouse with the peculiarly holy smell old houses have, a smell I'd always imagined to be somehow associated with the generations of births and deaths they've witnessed, but which I've recently been told is to do with the lichen-like growth on old stones. There were log fires in every grate.

There was winter jasmine in our room, and champagne. The bed was huge and high and ravishingly cold and each morning when we pulled back the curtains, we found they'd laid on a pretty peppering of snow, just enough for effect, not enough to stop us going out. Not that we did go out, but we wouldn't have wanted any petty restrictions. What we did was to stay in, sitting close together, reading old magazines, *Country Life* and *Gloucestershire Times*, and talking and drinking champagne. What exercise we got was certainly not from country walks.

It was a quiet hotel, only eight people staying, and though they'd had twenty people in to Christmas lunch and were expecting forty-five on New Year's Eve, when we were there it was delightfully quiet and sober. Our fellow guests were elderly and charming, and apart from conversation with the afternoon tea and mince pies, liked to be left alone to doze and dream and watch old films on television.

Lovely days, so cold and short, lovely nights so warm and long. I probably didn't deserve any of it, but I got it. The Feast of Stephen.

But in the new year, when I thought it was all plain sailing, he had to go to Japan for ten days, and as soon as he'd gone I found myself tortured by fears that I would never see him again. Ten days seemed an endlessly long rope to be hauled in minute by slow minute. Sometimes I would wake in the night and wonder if I had imagined him, he seemed too good and kind and loving to be true. If he died in Japan, I would only hear of it casually, through Walter. 'Frightful thing, Tessa, you'll never believe it, Fielding had a heart attack in Japan; died before they got him to hospital.' I wasn't even his next of kin. I imagined train disasters and plane disasters, hurricanes and earthquakes. I imagined him in the grip of secret agents or geisha girls. I even dreamed of separation and death and then woke and cried and read love poetry and was short-tempered with the children all day. When John rang at the end of the week to make arrangements to have the children, he was worried about me, even my voice over the telephone was different. 'Are you sure you're all right?' he asked, two or three times, so that I finally explained to him what the matter was. 'I'm in love, that's all,' I said. 'It's hell, isn't it,' he said gloomily.

Victor was due back at Heathrow early on Sunday morning. I wanted to turn up to meet him, but I was afraid that his wife might be there. I was awake before five hoping that he'd phone from the airport, but he didn't. He wouldn't want to wake me, I told myself, but I wasn't comforted. He should have wanted to wake me.

I checked that the plane had landed. It had. I couldn't get back to sleep.

He still hadn't phoned at eleven.

I told myself that he'd have gone to bed and would drive over in the afternoon. By two-thirty I was striding about the sitting-room, wringing the handkerchief I'd got for the purpose and throwing cushions about. At four-thirty I had given up hope and was trying to decide what to do with the rest of my life.

At about seven o'clock he phoned.

'When did you get back?' I asked feebly.

'Early this morning, before six.' He sounded tired, dispirited, distant.

Fear made me distant, too. 'Did you have a good time?'

'Of course I didn't have a good time. I didn't go for a good time.'

I wondered what else I could say. I didn't say anything. I wondered if the conversation would struggle to its feet again or whether we would just hold on for ever, listening to the silence growing deeper between us.

'Shall I come over on Tuesday night?' he said at last. (When before had he ever asked about coming?)

'Yes, that would be nice.' I was already clutching at straws.

No longer shocked that he wasn't coming before then, only grateful that he intended coming at all.

On Tuesday morning, he telephoned to say he couldn't make it that evening, that he would come on Thursday. He was ringing from the office, he sounded very busy, said he had no time to talk. So I washed my hair on Tuesday evening and waited for Thursday. In those few days I learned that I'd clutch at anything, accept anything.

But on Thursday he seemed more or less back to normal and I put his bad mood down to jet-lag and fatigue.

It was about two months later that he told me that it was on that Sunday that he had told Elspeth about me. 'I didn't want you to worry about it,' he said. 'It had to be done.'

Looking back, I'm pleased that I had such an agonizing few days.

At the end of January, he bought a house for us, not far from the Common where we used to lie on those summer evenings, and we lived there, and still live there, together. We moved in on March 21st, officially the first day of spring, which seemed another good omen. It was built in the twenties and is large and inconvenient and of a dark and dubious character, mock Tudor; leaded lights and beams. We often talk of moving, but the garden is secluded and pretty and it's near Dora's school and the Common is so close that we don't have to take Daisy for walks. We're not house-proud, any of us. I'd always felt vaguely ashamed that the old faded curtains which came with the house are still on the windows, but quite recently a fashionable friend fingered them and said, 'Antique velvet, how super.' Perhaps the whole house is on the way up. I've got a feeling that we'll be here to see its rise or fall.

Two years and two weeks after moving in, we got married. I became Tessa Fielding, instead of Tessa Jilks, which sounds much better. There was no change in our relationship; it couldn't improve and didn't deteriorate.

Other things happened as well. I did my teachers' training. Dear Miss Hammond, though, had retired before I started it.

However, it was she who interviewed me, in the same grey cardigan and still eager for me to do Junior Mathematics.

I taught French in a Mixed Comprehensive School for three years. I wasn't a marvellous teacher but I enjoyed it and I don't think I put many kids off the subject, which is something. I had trouble with discipline, but not much more than anyone else. Gone are the days, thank goodness, when children jump to attention when a teacher comes into a room; all the same, I was never entirely happy at the wolf-whistles and glad little cries which greeted my entrance. However, I used to smile brightly, raise my hand and flutter my fingers, then sit at my desk, yanking my skirt down as far as it would go over my knees and plunge into French conversation which silenced most of them.

One of the things I enjoyed most about teaching was the counselling I did; this was the subsidiary subject I did in my training year, and in my second year's teaching, I did about four sessions a week.

Mrs Watkinson, a capable motherly teacher in her early fifties, was the official counsellor and she saw the girls with the tough problems like a father in prison or VD. I saw some of the others, those with personality problems; no one liked them, no one loved them, they had no friends, no interests. I couldn't help them much, of course, but I listened and tried to remember what they'd said, even names, so that they knew I was concerned.

Easier to deal with were those with unhappy or too intense love-affairs. I thought I was fairly good with those, very easily shocked, which was one of the things they liked. Don't rush into an engagement, I used to say, just to get a ring or something – they didn't know what I was talking about – don't rush into marriage without doing everything else as well, don't rush into it as though you've been offered a great prize. Love is the great prize, not marriage. Look about you, I used to say, play the field, take your time.

It's easy to advise. I loved it. Only two men ever proposed to me and I married both of them. One could have been chosen for me by computer, so well-matched were our tastes and outlooks and opinions, and after five years we were dead to each other; marriage had left us stranded like empty shells at high tide.

The second marriage, based on physical attraction, seems to be doing pretty well up to now.

There are so many broken marriages and broken trial-marriages and discarded affairs about, that young people are getting cynical about love, and that's the most dangerous thing of all. Falling in love is still the safest bet, I think.

Postscript

And after the brash, psychedelic sixties, the sinking seventies, pinched sobriety which even Jubilee was not quite able to dispel. However, we survived.

Victor is a little fatter and greyer, but much the same; even-tempered and indulgent to all of us. He complains a great deal about the financial situation as all rich men do (he laughs when I call him a rich man, but he certainly is by my standards), and drinks too much and is more and more engrossed in his work. He still takes me out on Friday nights, but when occasionally I let him off he seems pleased. Getting him to take a holiday, too, is increasingly difficult, though we did manage a few days in Brittany this year. (I shouldn't speak disparagingly of it. It was lovely. We were on our own and I fancied him all the time.)

Dora is very beautiful. Fifteen. So slender she seems to be swaying, and with eyes which are clear blue like scyllas. She's not very fond of me this year but it doesn't seem to be breaking my heart. I'm quite prepared for a one-sided relationship. I can't see why children should love their parents with the intensity their parents love them. The truth is that they only love us wholeheartedly until they're six or seven and I suppose that's as it should be.

The person Dora worships is John's wife, giving a new twist to all the fairy stories which, stiffened with boredom and tired to the bone, I used to read to her night after night after night.

John remarried two years ago. His wife is called Jaqui. She looks about seventeen in the wedding photograph Dora keeps prominently displayed in her room, though she must be rather older since she had, according to Dora, a First at Cambridge.

Toby doesn't seem quite as keen on her. When John was single, Toby used to be allowed to get his own meals in the flat, baked beans and beef-burgers and tinned custard, but in the new dispensation he's given health foods and salad. But

Toby is his own man; he doesn't place adult affection very high on his list of priorities. A few years ago when Dora was at a, thankfully brief, anti-Victor stage, 'He's not my father, Daddy's my father,' Toby looked at her and asked, 'Who's mine?' 'Daddy, you idiot. Don't you care about anything?' 'No.'

Still, she must be rather kind, Jaqui. When Dora told her that Claudia wanted to come for a weekend, she immediately wrote to invite her, and now she's been several times.

Claudia is six. Victor's baby. Plump and fair and lazy like me, gentle like him. Victor almost had a nervous breakdown over her birth, though it was easy and straightforward in every way. He used to take time off work to come with me to my ante-natal examinations, and because he was told on one occasion that I was slightly anaemic, was convinced that I was going to die and used to wake me at night asking how I felt. For a time I had to give up being a vegetarian; not for my health nor for the baby's, but for his. I wouldn't have done that for anyone else.

Claudia looked like a pink and white china doll even on the first day; the first hour. 'She looks so young,' Victor kept telling everyone who came near. They thought he meant me and smiled at him, but he meant the baby. It had unnerved him to find that he was so much older than all the other fathers; I think he feared that she might look – not exactly middle-aged and grey-haired – but certainly mature.

I was afraid that he would be a besotted father and indeed he is. I don't think Dora and Toby mind too much though, since his devotion to Claudia often takes the form of little personal attentions like washing behind her ears and cutting her toenails, things I've never been over-scrupulous about.

My mother and father celebrated their ruby wedding last year. They're both very fit. Barbara is a Professor and David, her husband, has become something of a television personality; his lectures on the diseases of the bladder and the intestines having unexpectedly hit the charts, so that he's my mother's number one at the moment, though she still finds my father amusing.

John's mother did get married, but unfortunately I never met Harry. She cut off relations with me when John and I split up. Lately, however, she's been asking after me, so perhaps we'll meet again one day. Harry is one of the few people who Toby reckons to be fond of. He's got a great sense of humour, he says. Toby goes off to them quite happily when Dora and Claudia go to John's, and then Victor and I have a lovely weekend on our own with old Daisy.

I'm not a perceptive person, I've often made wrong decisions and I'm constantly being surprised by events. I was completely taken in by Victor's apparent dislike of Daisy and once I'd registered that all his cursing did her no positive harm, it didn't bother me too much. It wasn't till she had a slight road accident a few years ago that I learned the truth, and it says a great deal for my love for Victor that I've never once referred to the extremely noisy and embarrassing demonstration he made in the Vet's surgery. I never even smile in a meaningful way when, five or six times a week, he says that she's the worst thing that ever happened to him.

Poor old Daisy is fat and slow now, but she's still a supah dog.

We still see quite a lot of Carole and Walt. They adopted another baby last year; it was nine years before Carole felt ready for the second. She washed Timothy's face in cool boiled water for nearly a year. She was told to do that when she first had him at ten days and no one told her to stop. Their second child is a little girl called Anna Maria and I am her godmother (as the boss's wife, Walt excused my lack of faith) and I'm very fond of her and intend to spoil her.

Ten years ago, I was awfully worried about the step I was taking. I worried about breaking with John, though he'd done everything but beg me to do so, I worried about John's mother and my own parents, and most of all about the effects on the children. They all pulled through without noticeable strain.

Yes, Dora is difficult (and so is Toby in a maddeningly placid and easy-going way), secretive, over-sensitive, rude, easily bored; but perhaps she would be just the same if John and I were still together. All her friends seem quite as awful; in my probably prejudiced opinion, worse. She is sometimes helpful and affectionate, Toby sometimes witty and companionable.

'Why ever did you marry Victor?' Dora asked me a few weeks ago, bitter about some recent altercation (acceptable noise levels, hours?). 'Was it just for his money?'

I was framing a suitably crushing reply when Toby leaned towards us, showing uncharacteristic interest. 'Or was it sex?' he asked. 'He is a bit, sort of . . . sometimes, isn't he?'

He obviously feared he'd gone too far. 'Lovey-dovey,' he said lamely.

'And he's very kind,' Claudia said. She left her drawing-board to join us.

Her presence turned the inquisition into a game.

'And he has his hair cut and he shuts doors and he doesn't interrupt her,' Toby said.

'And he laughs at her jokes,' Dora said, 'and says, "Listen to your mother."'

'And he's very clever at finding things, too,' Claudia said. 'He's found the winder of my watch about a million times.'

'And always takes her side on every possible occasion.'

'Without even listening to the argument.'

There was a moment's silence which seemed like a truce. We smiled at one another.

'What is sex?' Claudia asked, then.

'It's what mummies and daddies do when they're alone together,' Toby told her. He was about to elaborate, but Claudia had it in one.

'Oh, I know. When they want you to go downstairs for breakfast and they say, "I wonder if Snoopy's any good today."'

'I wonder if Snoopy's any good today!' Toby coloured and giggled and rolled off the sofa.

'Sometimes they say, "Won't Emily be waiting for you, darling?"'

'I wonder if old Snoopy's . . . !' Toby threshed about on the floor like a grounded fish and Claudia got a bit above herself.

'Sometimes they say –' she closed her eyes and yawned – ' "Let Mummy and Daddy have a bit more sleep, sweetheart." Sometimes they just say, "Push off now, Claudy." '

By this time she was sitting on Toby's chest, tickling and biting him, and even Dora had joined in, kissing Claudia on the back of her neck and laughing; the original question answered and forgotten.

On the whole, the children seem all right. I needn't have worried.

The only person I didn't worry about was Victor's wife, Elspeth. I didn't know anything about her and didn't want to. I felt she was Victor's responsibility, that I had enough on my plate.

By this time, though, I think about her a great deal. I still know very little about her. Victor rings her from time to time because she's a shareholder in one of his companies, but he never talks about her. Once she phoned him and I answered. She sounded a nice person; gentle. She hasn't remarried.

How easy it would be if she had rung me and abused me, if she had done something really bitchy so that I could dislike and despise her. But she did nothing, does nothing, nothing but exist quietly without Victor. Perhaps she didn't love him and was pleased to be free. Perhaps she's never quite got over his leaving her. I think about her.

I've always hated the parable of the talents. How could the man who spoke with such idealistic scorn of the rich, come out with the sickening materialism of that parable? 'Thou wicked and slothful servant, thou knewest that I reap where I sowed not and gather where I have not strawed . . . Take therefore the talent from him, and give it unto him which hath ten talents. For unto every one that hath shall be given, and he shall have abundance : but from him that hath not shall be taken away even that which he hath.' Horrible. Don't think that I don't worry about it.

Sometimes I blame Victor for deserting her; how could he have decided so quickly to leave his wife of sixteen years for a girl he'd known only for three or four months; and have to make excuses for him. He makes rapid decisions. It's his business training; that's what makes one successful in business perhaps, not making necessarily the right decision, but any one as long as it's fast and authoritative.

I see it work with Dora and Toby and even little Claudia.

May she, Dora asks, sleep at a friend's house after the party on Saturday night. What party? What friend? I spend a long time with searching enquiries and finally decide that I wouldn't be happy about it. I'm desperately sorry. Dora then weighs in with several more arguments to support her request and I hesitate. 'Ask Victor,' I say.

When he comes in, she does.

'No,' he says. 'Absolutely not. Ask again when you're sixteen.'

Toby wants to go to a film which I know to be sordid and tasteless. I point this out to him. I remind him of the poor reviews it had, what so-and-so said in such-and-such. I suggest another film, also dirty, but well-reviewed. Toby wouldn't go to see that, of course, even if I paid him.

'Oh, ask Victor,' I say.

'Yes, by all means. Sounds like a great film. I'd come with you if I had the time. Why don't you take your mother along?'

Claudia agonizes about whether to buy Sweet Mary Lou who walks and talks or Baby Blue Eyes who kisses and dribbles and wets her nappy. I'm nervous about being drawn into such delicate matters. I may know which is likely to last, but what do I know about the factors influencing her: which does Emily Patterson have, which appears more frequently on the telly ads, which doesn't Emily Patterson have.

'This one,' Victor says, hardly glancing at them. 'This is the best.' He picks it up and pays for it and she follows him out of the shop, entirely happy.

I suppose that's how it was ten years ago when he chose me. 'This one.' With hardly a second glance.

Why should I worry, I say to myself, I got him. It was either her or me. All the same, I worry.

So that's it; the summing up. I'm not claiming to be blissfully or ecstatically happy. It would be presumptuous and foolish and courting disaster, anyway; the film-stars who tell the glossy magazines how happy they are this year, are next year having trial separations, would be having divorces except that they're not, this year, having marriages; what I will say is that I'm pretty happy quite a lot of the time.

And almost all the time I feel alive and glad to be alive; my life is full. The older children may not need me as much as they did but, as long as I don't interfere too much, usually seem pleased to have me around. And I'm still as necessary to Claudia as air and cornflakes. The house doesn't interest me much but I'm becoming a keen gardener. I don't grow vegetables or make compost, self-sufficiency isn't my scene, what I do is collect old plants, particularly old roses. My gallicas are worth seeing.

I teach at Night School two evenings a week, mostly holiday French, which is quite enjoyable if not exactly stimulating.

And with various friends I go to concert and opera and theatre and art gallery. I've become almost the intellectual Victor took me for ten years ago.

Occasionally I invite my highbrow friends to dinner and while we discuss all that's new, Victor looks on, smiling at us tolerantly. These people, I tell myself, seek out and support what is best in art, while he is a materialist of narrow vision and little sensibility; for things of the mind having no regard. Even as I say it, I know it's nonsense.

He reads books, even if he doesn't read reviews. Yes, he knows what pictures he likes, too, and why should that be mocked, to me it seems far more laudable than to like what one has been taught is good taste. And if he's scathing about most of what I take him to see in the cinema and the theatre, he will often be enraptured by something else, a documentary before the main film or something quite unpublicized on television, and it's never what he's been advised to like; what others rave about. He comes to his own conclusions. To me, he seems all right.

'I love you,' I said, as he came in tonight. I very rarely say it.

He looked tired, older than he did when he left this morning and he was nearly fifty then. He had a dark grey suit on, very much like the one he wore when I first saw him, a striped shirt, a light grey tie.

We stood together for a moment. He rested his hand on my arm, he has beautiful hands. 'Of course you do,' he said complacently. 'We settled all that.'